★

The rest rooms were in a narrow, dimly lit hallway leading to a door with a neon exit sign above it. The pay phone was right next to the men's room, just as Debbie had said. It had a shelf underneath and wings to either side, so someone using it had a modicum of privacy. And could easily remain anonymous. If anyone came back here to use either the men's or women's room while the call was being made, only the back of a coat would be visible.

I was about to return to the main room when a man's arm slammed across my chest, knocking the wind out of me.

"Goddamn it," a voice whispered in my ear. "Don't make me kill you."

★

"A powerful second mystery."

—*Library Journal*

Previously published Worldwide Mystery title by
CATHERINE DAIN

DEATH OF THE PARTY

FOLLOW THE MURDER

MURDER

CATHERINE DAIN

W🌐RLDWIDE®

TORONTO • NEW YORK • LONDON
AMSTERDAM • PARIS • SYDNEY • HAMBURG
STOCKHOLM • ATHENS • TOKYO • MILAN
MADRID • WARSAW • BUDAPEST • AUCKLAND

FOLLOW THE MURDER

A Worldwide Mystery/September 2003

First published by Five Star.

ISBN 0-373-26468-2

FOLLOW THE MURDER

ONE

"I'M SO GLAD you're a therapist, I can't find words to tell you how glad I am you're a licensed therapist," I said, plopping into a chair. The iron legs screeched against the stone floor as I shifted it around so that I wasn't facing the sun. "I need to decompress before I go back to the clinic and see my next client, and since you're a therapist we can call lunch a consultation, and I won't be violating confidence."

"My two remaining clients will be thrilled to know that I have joined the ranks of consulting therapist," Michael answered. "Can you stand to order first? I'm hungry."

"You could have more clients if you wanted them." I pulled out my reading glasses and picked up a menu, neither expecting nor finding radical changes since the last time I had eaten there.

Most people develop a need for reading glasses in their forties. I was one of the lucky few who needed them in her late thirties, something I discovered in graduate school when the fine type in textbooks began to bounce. Being told that the condition was called presbyopia, which means old man's eyes, depressed me for a week.

I put the menu down, put my glasses back in my bag, and looked at Michael. "Owning the spokescat for Pretty Kitty cat food has changed your priorities, that's all.''

"That's a nice way of saying I'm lazy, and thank you for that,'' Michael said. "Although Elizabeth believes she owns me, and I'm not disabusing her of the notion. I'm having the free-range chicken salad on rosemary bread, if that helps you decide.''

I had eaten at the restaurant often enough that I was familiar with the lunch choices. I glanced at the specials, tossed the menu aside, and looked around for someone to take our order.

The patio was filled with hungry people who wanted lunch in a hurry, and one young woman with a pony tail and an apron, both part of the standard L.A. server's uniform, was doing her best to keep everyone happy. Southern California has a bargain with the local weather god that the month of January will be seventy degrees and sunny, a fact one would expect restaurant owners with patios to remember when scheduling staff for lunch, but a surprising number forget. I settled back to wait.

Because Michael had asked me not to discuss my client until we ordered, I looked at him and smiled, lips tight.

"All right, Faith,'' he said, adding a sigh that Al Gore would have loved. "Tell me about your client.''

"She's clinically depressed,'' I answered.

"So is half the membership of the Screen Actors Guild.'' He was keeping one eye on the young woman's progress, and his right hand was raised, ready to flag her down.

When he succeeded, he beamed at me triumphantly.

I knew there was no point in talking until ordering lunch was accomplished. Taking care of his body was still one of Michael's priorities. He had that youthful-at-forty look that comes from a bargain with another of the local gods, the one in charge of physical beauty. So I allowed myself a moment to enjoy the sun and admire the patio, which was adorned with an eclectic mix of umbrellas, lush plants, and space heaters, there because the temperature would drop without warning after sunset.

"You ready to order?" the server asked, pad and pencil poised above us. She was too harried to smile.

"Cream of broccoli soup and the foccaccia with herbed olive oil," I said. "And iced tea."

Michael ordered his sandwich and iced tea and then turned both his eyes on me, eyebrows arched, waiting for an explanation.

"I know depression is common," I said. "Even crippling depression, the kind where the person doesn't get out of bed until after noon. I could handle hearing about that, although trying to get somebody living in a black cloud to talk to me about her problems for an hour every week isn't my idea of fun. The thing is, though, when she does talk about them, there's no affect in her voice. At first I thought she might be suicidal."

Michael looked dubious. "Has she threatened suicide? Suicide doesn't necessarily go with depression, you know."

"I know, and no, she hasn't threatened suicide. Quite the opposite. This morning she threatened to kill her ex-husband." I paused for dramatic effect. Michael politely raised his eyebrows. "Right now I think she's too emotionally fatigued to carry through. But her depression stems from her anger at him turned inward. The reason a lot more depressives don't commit suicide is that they don't have the energy. The dicey period, as you know, is when they start to get a little better, but their problems still seem impossible to handle. So suppose she starts to come out of her depression, gets a little energy, turns a lot more anger outward, and killing her ex-husband feels like a really good idea? You see my problem.''

"I do. If you do your legal duty and warn her ex-husband, you've betrayed her trust, and she has to start over with another therapist and a darker cloud. Not to mention a restraining order keeping her away from the ex.'' Michael was now interested. "On the other hand, if you don't warn him and she turns violent, you might lose your license.''

"And her ex-husband might be dead,'' I added.

"How serious did the threat sound?''

"Well, she wanted to watch him bleed to death, and she described the process in great detail, and with almost a hint of interest in her voice. It was an actual train of thought, the first I've heard her follow in four months of therapy,'' I told him. "On a serious scale of one to ten, I'd rate it maybe a five.''

"Best thing to do is buck the problem. Refer her to somebody else, somebody who can prescribe heavy duty drugs,'' Michael said.

"I could do that if she were a private patient, but she's a walk-in at the clinic. She doesn't have the money for a psychiatrist. She doesn't even have the money to pay me. And if I try to alert someone at the clinic, I'm doing the same thing as alerting her ex. I have to be sure first.''

Volunteering eight hours a week, four on Tuesday and four on Thursday, at a storefront medical clinic on Sunset Boulevard had seemed like a good idea when I was interning for my therapist's license, and I had continued even after because I could never bring myself to quit. At that moment I was sorry, feeling punished for my good intentions.

"Then you're stuck with her," Michael said, with a rare note of genuine compassion in his voice. "And you're going to have to assess the threat yourself, use your own judgment as to whether to warn her ex or report her to anyone else. Are you sure she's too depressed to act now?''

"Reasonably so. Her fantasies of hurting him haven't turned into the kind of plan anyone might act on.''

"Forgive my naiveté, but what kind of murderous plan might someone act on?'' he asked.

"Oh, you know, guns, knives, poisons, chain saws, even an ice pick in the heart," I said. "In her fantasy he came over to see her, bringing a bottle of wine as a peace offering, and she broke the bottle and jammed the jagged neck into his face, causing him to lose consciousness and bleed to death. I'm not sure what artery she could sever in his face that would cause him to bleed to death.''

"I gather you don't think the arrival of the ex with a peace offering is likely to begin with.''

"No." I paused while the young woman dropped our lunches on the table, slowing just long enough to let the plates settle before she was off to the next set of hungry patrons. "From what I can gather, they have no reason to be in touch with one another. She has two children, but those are teenagers from another marriage, so there are no custody issues or anything."

I broke off a hunk of the crusty foccaccia and dipped it in the herbed olive oil. The mix was just right.

"Any history of violence?" Michael asked.

"Not that I'm aware of," I said around the mouthful of bread.

"In that case, there's probably no harm in waiting a week or two. See if she brings it up again." Michael took a bite out of his sandwich.

"That's really what I had decided. I needed you to agree, though." I was beginning to relax. It's not music that soothes the savage breast, it's food.

"I agree. I also think they need a better reporting network at the clinic," Michael said between bites.

"You're right. Are you volunteering?"

He made gestures to indicate that he couldn't answer because his mouth was full.

Once it was clear, he said, "How's the new apartment?"

"Not as interesting as the old house, but a lot quieter and safer. The only noise in the night comes from my downstairs neighbor, who sounds like the woman Dr. Ruth applauds in the orgasmic shampoo commercial, and I don't know whether I should say something to her about it or not. It's really more intimacy than I'm ready for." I swallowed a spoonful of the rich soup. Michael's mouth was too full for him to comment. "No drug deals going down on the corner. No burglaries that I know of. It's a long drive to the clinic, though, and I haven't unpacked all my boxes because I'm not in love with Sherman Oaks, even south of the boulevard. The best I can say is, it'll do for now, at least until I decide about Richard.''

"That's still pending? I thought you said he renewed his lease when you moved to the Valley. And, silly me, I thought that meant things were cooling off." His eyebrows went up again. "Wasn't the original idea that you two would find a place together when his lease was up?"

"That was his idea. I said I needed more time, so he renewed his lease for six months. And I'm renting month to month, so I can move on thirty days' notice." I stopped for another spoonful of soup, and a piece of bread. "I just don't know whether I want to live with anyone right now, except Amy and Mac.''

"That means you don't want to live with anyone but the cats. How are they adjusting?''

"Oh, well, at least they're out from under the bed most of the time. They haven't yet realized that the deck is the limit of their territory. No more backyards to explore, no fences to climb, just cement and some potted plants.''

"Are you sure you can live with that?" Michael's mouth was partly full, and it came out a mumble. I knew what he meant, though. I had liked having a yard with flowering plants, and the pots on the deck just weren't the same.

"No. That's part of the problem, of course. No place to dig in the dirt. But more than that, I miss Silver Lake. I miss the mix of people. I miss funky.''

"I shudder at the thought." He did a silent screen star shudder, to illustrate. "But Silver Lake and Sherman Oaks aren't the only choices, you know, with or without Richard.''

"I know that, too," I said. "But this apartment opened up at the right time, and taking it seemed like a reasonable thing to do while Richard and I sort things out. I do love him.''

"But?''

The answer to that was going to be long enough that I made Michael wait while I sopped up more olive oil with the focaccia and ate it.

"But I always seem to get involved with men who suck up all the energy in the room," I said, "and while that's great fun when you're having an affair, I'm not certain I could live with it. Or at least not as an adult—I was hardly more than a child the one time I tried. The thing is, two days with Richard and I want to go home and recover.''

"Then you can't live with him." Michael said it as if that made everything simple. "But if you can work out the logistics, separate apartments in the same city might be a civilized arrangement for as long as the passion lasts.''

"I could make a good case for it. I'm not sure he can. He seems to regard separate apartments as something less than a total commitment." I didn't wait for Michael to slip in an obvious response. "He even suggested that I might have intimacy issues.''

"Which you do, of course." He managed to make one anyway.

"Well, in some ways, maybe. But there are good reasons why I'm feeling shy of total commitment right now," I said, hoping I didn't sound too defensive. "I just don't want to discuss them with Richard."

"Ouch. That's the relationship killer, Faith."

"I don't see why we can't see each other when we want to, enjoy each other's company, and then do whatever else we want to do," I argued. "That works with you."

"We're friends," he pointed out. "There's a difference between friends and lovers. Richard wants more than friendship with sex. You apparently don't. When are you going to make that clear to him?"

"I suspect it already is. In any case, I'm going to a gallery opening with him tomorrow night. Some friend of his is having her first exhibit. I'll be surprised if we make it through the evening without some sort of major discussion of living arrangements."

Michael shook his head. "Think before you end this. Richard does have many fine qualities, you know."

"When did he stop being the crazy artist and start having fine qualities?" I asked, genuinely surprised.

"When he gave me the portrait of Elizabeth for Christmas, of course." Michael had finished his sandwich, and he pushed his plate away. "I didn't realize he had the craftsmanship to carry off a parody of *The Birth of Venus*."

"I'll rephrase that before I tell him how much you loved the gift," I said, pushing back my own plate. "I'm sorry to eat and run, but I do have to get back. Is there anything going on in your life that I need to know about?"

"I am blessed with the freedom to contemplate existence," he said.

"In other words, you need a hobby," I replied. "Use it or lose it applies to the mind, you know."

He sniffed, and the sniff turned into a sneeze. The Santa Ana condition that brings seventy degree weather in January also brings wet noses and dry hair.

"Bless you," I said.

"Thank you," he replied. "And I'll think about a hobby. Good luck with your afternoon clients."

"These are problems I can deal with—one was burned out of her apartment, lost all her things, and the other was in an auto accident, her fault, no insurance, and she's being sued for every dime she has, which isn't many. Straightforward grief in both cases, although number two is having a little problem accepting responsibility." I reached for the check, but Michael grabbed it and held it away from the table. "Thanks. I'll talk to you soon."

I worked my way through the tables to the sidewalk, and from there to the parking lot, to get my blue Taurus. I was ready for air conditioning, which I had in my car, but wouldn't have in my office. With the price of electricity sky high, the clinic had discontinued everything unnecessary, and someone decided that meant air conditioning in January. My contribution to my own sanity was an oscillating fan.

The restaurant was on Hillhurst, in Los Feliz Village, one of those collections of quaint shops that appear magically out of the jumble of L.A. It was a few blocks north of Sunset, and the clinic was only a couple of miles east of that junction, near where Silver Lake became Echo Park. Actually, the clinic was little more than a minimall storefront with four tiny offices, shared by three family doctors and two volunteer therapists.

Nominally, of course, I should have discussed my client not with Michael, but with the family doctor who headed the clinic. She always seemed too busy to focus, though, and I didn't want to drop anything more on her desk than I had to.

Michael was right. The thing to do was to see if the fantasy of violence recurred.

I parked the Taurus right in front of the clinic, pleased that the local parking god had smiled on me.

"Oh, good, you're on time," Mary said in greeting, after she had buzzed me in. Casual visitors tended to be distracted by her spiked burgundy hair and the small gold loops attached to her nose and eyebrows, but those of us who worked there knew that the bilingual receptionist was the one indispensable person in the clinic.

"I am. Where's Luisa?" Luisa was my client, the woman whose apartment had been gutted in a fire that began in her neighbor's kitchen.

"Waiting in your office. With the fan on and the window open, it's the coolest place for her to sit."

I shook my head in comment and walked back to my office. The reception area had its own fan, of course, but the afternoon sun was beating in, and for safety reasons the windows couldn't be opened. The door had been locked and equipped with a buzzer after a homeless person had wandered in and threatened Mary. She had handled it well, staying calm until one of the doctors came out of his office, but we had all agreed that precautions had to be taken.

Luisa, it turned out, was perking up. She had heard from a lawyer who thought they could sue the building owner. I sat down to listen.

After Luisa came my last appointment of the day, the one already in a lawsuit. She was still bummed out, but coping, starting to deal with the situation.

I was feeling pretty good when I left the clinic, good enough that I remembered to think about food for dinner before I got on the Hollywood Freeway for the slow drive through the Cahuenga Pass to the Valley. L.A. is a great place to live for those of us who love to eat and hate to cook, because so many other people are willing to do it for us, thus creating what was once the oxymoron of gourmet take-out.

About three blocks west and four blocks north of the clinic was one of my favorites, a tiny place with a few tables on an enclosed patio, no liquor license, and great crayfish etouffee. I was in and out and on my way again in ten minutes.

My new apartment was on the second floor of a two-story building erected after someone's mansion had been torn down. Whether the someone had been famous or just rich was a matter of argument around the swimming pool, a gym-sized beauty left from the original estate. It would have been easy enough to research if anyone really cared, but the participants preferred to argue.

I walked into a quiet apartment. No cats in sight. Or at least not in the large room that served as a combination living room, dining room, and office.

The office part was closest to the entrance, a desk with computer and phone. I had hung a reproduction of one of those great Maxfield Parrish women over the desk, a picture that always cheered me when I saw it. I hoped it would do the same for clients.

A sofa and an overstuffed chair, both in a fading pattern left over from when Santa Fe was chic, were part of the office, because I used them for clients, and part of the living room, because friends sat there, too. Two bookcases acted as a space divider, and beyond them sat a pine table with four chairs.

"Hey, babies," I called when I reached the table and still didn't see any cats.

Amy peered around the edge of the bedroom door. She stalked past me to the nook designed as an efficiency kitchen and stopped to stare accusingly. Amy was always put out about something, and she hadn't yet forgiven me for the move. Mac, her boy, trotted after, although he couldn't master the accusing stare. Aside from attitude, Mac looked just like his mother, both large cats with full, sable-colored coats.

The apartment was warm, so I detoured to open the sliding door to the deck on my way to the kitchen. Mac dashed out, tail waving like a plume, then dashed back, when he realized I was popping the top to a can of cat food.

Once the cats were eating, I poured myself a glass of wine and checked my answering machine. No messages, which was good because it meant I had no emergencies to deal with, not so good in that I had spent a lot of money on the move, and I could use a couple of referrals.

I took the glass of wine out to the deck and stretched out on the redwood chaise longue, my favorite spot in the apartment. The view was mostly trees, with bits and pieces of nearby apartment houses showing through. I liked it—almost my own tree house.

Amy hopped up by my feet and started giving herself a bath. Mac followed five seconds later. They really considered the blue-and-white striped cushion theirs, although they were willing to share it with me.

Would I be happier living with Richard?

Probably not.

I spent a quiet evening with the cats, the wine, the crayfish etouffee, and a book that was too good to put down.

In the morning, the quiet was shattered by a phone call.

"Can you come in to the clinic?" Mary asked. "Natalie Thorson is here, and she says she has to talk to you."

"Now? I just saw her yesterday."

"But last night her ex-husband was murdered."

I almost dropped the phone.

"I'll be there in an hour. Don't let her leave."

I closed my eyes. This was too heavy for a local god. I prayed to a Bigger One that my client wasn't a murderer.

TWO

"I DIDN'T DO IT," Natalie shrieked, rocking back and forth in the frayed armchair. She was wide-eyed and disheveled, wearing a dirty T-shirt and jeans, with limp, oily brown hair hanging around her white face, but she was no longer depressed. "And the police are going to blame me, I know they are."

The day before, everything about Natalie had been muted. I would have sworn she was so depressed she could barely function. But her ex-husband's murder had shattered the numbness that had lain like a coat of ice over her emotions. His ill wind had at least blown her some good. Not that I wasn't sorry for him—no one deserves to be murdered. Nevertheless, she was my client, he wasn't, and he had put her through a lot.

"Why would the police blame you?" I asked, hoping I didn't already know the answer.

"The message I left on his answering machine," she said, still shrieking.

"What did the message say?" My voice had the calm, even tones of a professional, although my heart was pounding.

"That I wanted to kill him, of course." Natalie stopped shrieking and began to sob. Her words came out in short jerks. "It felt so good, leaving that message. I felt good. I felt good for the first time in months, felt as if I had the strength to do something, even if it was only leaving a message on Craig's machine. And then somebody else killed him."

"How do you feel about that?" I asked. It's one of those questions you think you shouldn't have to ask, but you do.

"I am so angry," she said, pounding her knee with her fist. "I am so angry that I was finally starting to get in touch with my feelings about that jerk, thinking I could work through the rage and maybe I could even gain control of my life, and now he's dead. How can he be dead?"

I had no answer to that, so I did my best to look wise, and waited for her to continue.

"I wasn't really going to kill Craig, you know," she said, not even concerned that I hadn't answered her. "I just wanted him to be scared. I wanted to have some power over him, to affect him, because he had so much power over me for so long. And now he's dead."

Her voice rose to a wail.

"Do you know how it happened?" I asked.

"The police didn't give me many details." She stopped crying and looked at me through bloodshot eyes. "That's another reason I think they may suspect me. All they said was, Craig was murdered, somebody stabbed him in the kitchen, and they wanted to know where I was last night."

"And you told them…" I prompted.

"That I was home. I was." Her face twisted as she said it, but her voice stayed steady.

"With Jimmy and Sarah?"

"No. Jimmy was with his girlfriend. I have no control over him, and I wish he were seeing someone else, but he isn't. The two of them talk about finding a place together, but then, of course, one of them would have to get a job." Natalie blinked and shook her head, apparently realizing she was getting off-track. "And Sarah went over to stay with my mother. Mom thought I needed a good night's sleep, and she said she would get Sarah to school this morning. I haven't even told them what's happened."

The day before I would have agreed with her mother. Now I was afraid she needed a lot more than that. Natalie had threatened to kill her ex and she had no alibi. What did they call that—motive and opportunity.

"You didn't go over to Craig's apartment or anything, did you?" I asked.

"Oh, Faith, you don't think I did it, do you?"

"No, Natalie. Of course I don't think you did it." And that was true. My memory of her depression was still too sharp. Unfortunately, I also remembered my concern over her threat of violence. I had thought she was too depressed to act, and now I had to consider whether I was wrong. The woman in front of me was capable of action. "But I couldn't help wondering if the police could tie you to the crime scene."

Natalie's jaw dropped.

When she had it back under control, she said, "You think the police are going to arrest me."

"I hope they don't, Natalie. Truly. I hope they don't." I took a breath. "Now, go back to the beginning. Tell me about the message you left."

"All it said, really, was that I hated him and wanted him dead and if God didn't strike him down with lightning, I might do it myself," Natalie said earnestly. "I didn't say anything specific, not how or anything like that."

"Nothing about wanting to watch him bleed to death?" I asked.

"I don't think so," she hedged. "I mean, I don't remember exactly what I said."

I didn't believe her.

"Did you mean it when you said it?" I asked.

"Sort of," she admitted. "Not really. I wanted to scare him, I told you, that was all. I had this fantasy that he'd be scared of me. I thought he might even call me, beg me not to kill him, or something like that."

One tear rolled unheeded down her cheek.

"But he didn't call you," I said, again prompting her to continue.

"No. Then this morning, two police officers knocked on my door. They said somebody stabbed Craig in the kitchen." Natalie paused. Evidently this time she said it, the absurdity hit her. "Well, stabbed him in the chest. With a kitchen knife."

"Did they say anything about suspects?"

"No, not exactly. They asked me where I was, and they asked me whether I knew of anybody else who might want to hurt Craig." Natalie hugged herself and started rocking again. "That was what scared me, that they said anybody else who might want to hurt him. So they had decided I did, I wanted to hurt him. So I told them I didn't mean it, didn't really plan to kill him, but I'm not sure they believed me.''

"Okay, but if your fingerprints had been on the knife, or anything like that, they would have arrested you. I mean, they have to have something more than the answering machine message before you're a serious suspect." I was trying to reassure myself as well as Natalie.

The tears flooded down her cheeks.

"I didn't tell them," she said, between sobs and gasps for breath, "and I didn't want to tell you, but I drove by Craig's apartment last night, when he didn't call me, drove by to see if he was home. The lights were on, and I didn't stop. I swear. And I went straight back home. But what if somebody saw my car?''

The rest of the hour didn't get any better.

I did my best to calm Natalie, promised to be available if she needed me, and urged her to let Sarah stay with her mother as long as she could. Jimmy was nineteen, out of school and unemployed, and Natalie hadn't been able to control him for some time. Sarah was only fifteen, though, and from what Natalie had told me, was doing okay. I had felt for a while that she had a better chance of staying okay if she stayed away from Natalie, and this was a good opportunity to give Sarah a break. Natalie was still crying when she left the clinic, but she seemed to be coping with the situation. She promised to call her mother, let her know what happened, and call me if any of them needed help.

I had done the best I could, and in any case, I didn't have time to worry about Natalie. I also didn't have time to worry about my own possible culpability if she had killed Craig. I had to rush home to get ready to see two clients in the afternoon, both women who were dealing with marriages who were falling apart. I was pretty much limiting my private practice to women, because my office was in my apartment, and I didn't like inviting unknown, possibly disturbed, men to the place where I lived. Renting office space to accommodate the possibility of male clients was something I had considered, but hadn't yet acted on.

That particular Friday, however, I was going to be doing a lot of driving. Sherman Oaks to the clinic, then the clinic to Sherman Oaks, then back to Silver Lake to meet Richard for dinner and the gallery showing.

I hadn't mentioned it to Michael because I didn't want to add it to the lunch menu, but it had occurred to me that part of the tension in my relationship with Richard had to do with his apartment, that whenever I drove over there, I relived the disasters of the dead bodies in the street.

Late that afternoon, I steeled myself to do it one more time. I put enough food down for the cats to last the night and slipped out of the house while Amy's face was in the food dish, to avoid the accusatory stare.

And I found myself dealing with a surge of annoyance, that Richard hadn't been more affected by the presence of violent death, even though I knew I had been closer to the people involved than he had, and certainly other people who lived on that street had chosen to stay. Not all of them. I hadn't been the only one to move. But he had stayed, and I had to drive back there to see him.

I had to force myself to calm down enough to drive safely.

By the time I had retraced my way through Cahuenga Pass and hit the welcome-to-the-inner-city traffic jam at the Melrose exit, I had given way to the annoyance. I got off the Hollywood Freeway at Benson Avenue, took the twists and turns through the old neighborhood to get to his apartment, and discovered I was angry all over again. All I could see was how rundown everything was, how many windows had bars, how many doors had security screens, how much graffiti was sprayed on the fences and the garage doors. At least I was no longer nostalgic for funky.

I parked my car on the street and hoped it would be all right. The wrought iron gate that should have protected the driveway to the small complex where Richard lived was broken again anyway, and stood open, so parking off the street wouldn't have helped much. And the crumbling fountain in front of the building was still overgrown with weeds. No attempt at maintenance. I tried to remember when this had seemed romantic to me, when it had reminded me of Raymond Chandler's L.A. It was hard.

And I tried to remind myself that it wasn't Richard's fault that my one-time boyfriend had deteriorated into a druggie who got shot in front of Richard's door.

I didn't care. It was Richard's fault that he still lived in that apartment.

I walked up the stairs and pounded on the door.

My anger faded a little when he opened it.

The lines around his soft blue eyes, maybe. The shaggy dark hair streaked with gray, the three day growth, the paint-stained sweat shirt, I don't know. Certainly the smile that cut dimples into a face best described as craggy. Something about him, when I was with him, made me want to curl up and purr.

"I'm running late, Faith," he said. "Come on in, pour yourself a glass of wine, and I'll hurry."

He always ran late. I accepted that as part of his charm. I grabbed him and kissed him lightly before he could run away.

"I'll skip the wine until dinner," I said.

Richard didn't drink, but he kept a bottle for me.

He kissed me back, then pulled away.

"If you don't let me take a shower, we won't have time for dinner," he warned.

"Go!" I said. "Go now! I need dinner."

"Rough day?"

I nodded. "I'll tell you later."

He trotted off to the shower, and I went on into his living room, which doubled as a studio, to see what he was working on.

The canvas on his easel showed a rough sketch of the minimall, including the clinic, the Mexican grocery store, and the Cuban bakery. A Polaroid snapshot was propped against one corner. I wondered when he had taken it. He hadn't really started to paint yet, so I couldn't tell what he planned on doing. There were some figures pencilled in, but nothing that would even let me know whether one was supposed to be me.

Other than that one canvas, and some sketches of the minimall on the floor beneath the easel, only a couple of paintings leaning against the wall and a battered cabinet full of art supplies identified the room as a work area.

Large floor pillows were all that identified the room as a living area.

Richard's neatness always amazed me. If I had been painting, there would have been wall-to-wall splatters instead of polished hardwood.

The view from the window that brought in bright, northwest light during the day always amazed me, too. A panorama, stretching from the Hollywood sign in the hills across several miles of tiny houses in the basin. In theory, one could see all the way to the ocean. In practice, the ocean was too far. The setting sun had turned the clouds bright red, reminding me that no matter how clear the day had seemed, there were still unhealthy particles in the air.

I could track Richard's progress through the noises from the water pipes, shower on, shower off. Getting dressed meant clean jeans and T-shirt, topped by leather jacket. I had long ago stopped wearing anything but jeans when I was with Richard, although I had gone for a lavender silk blouse and chunky gold jewelry in honor of the art gallery opening.

He was back and ready to go before I was tired of the view.

"Did you have something in mind for dinner?" he asked, knowing there were several restaurants in the area that I had enjoyed when I lived there.

"Chilean sea bass, although I've read that it's really Patagonian toothfish, and endangered, so this is the last time I eat it," I said. "Grab the wine."

"Thank God you're around to keep me politically correct. I somehow missed the story. The broiler or the Mexican place?" He was already on his way to the kitchen to get the wine, because neither place had a liquor license. Both were strictly bring-your-own.

"If we go to the broiler we'll have to wait in line," I answered. "So the Mexican place."

The Mexican place would be crowded, too, but the broiler on Friday night would be impossible.

When he came back with the wine, almost bouncing with good humor, he took my hand for a moment, squeezed it, and said, "Let's go."

I had planned on staying upset for a while, at least for as long as it took to tell him I had problems at work, but he was too cheerful. By the time we reached my car—I wasn't going to be caught on his Harley at night in January—I was almost bouncing, too, just glad to be in his presence.

We had to drive by the house where I used to live in order to get back to Sunset. The new tenant obviously didn't like working in the yard, and I felt momentarily sad about the decay, then just glad I didn't live there any longer.

The Mexican place was small, funky, crowded, and the sea bass was great. We didn't linger, and we didn't talk much because he wanted to get to the gallery. And I overlooked the fact that he had already forgotten to ask me about my rough day.

The art gallery was small, funky, crowded, and I hated his friend's work so much that I could hardly keep my mouth shut and smile. The paintings were pseudo-portraits, drawn the way a child might draw, with a few words of bad poetry sketched in around the edges of the heads.

It didn't help that, as usual with Richard, this friend was a woman in her twenties, one Cydnee DuPree. She was draped in something that looked like all seven of Salome's veils, each of them slip-sliding to one side of her body or the other. I could understand why women were attracted to Richard, even women half his age, or especially women half his age. But when Cydnee attached herself to his arm and dragged him around the exhibit, making a point of excluding me, I began to feel annoyed for the nth time that day.

When he didn't seem to notice I was excluded, I started to seethe. I was on my third glass of a cheap, sweet champagne that I normally would have scorned, ignoring a conversation between two art groupies about how Cydnee's work reflected the essential playfulness of the existential condition, before he came looking for me.

"I guess you want to leave," he said, with a half smile that would have looked good on a teenage prankster.

"I guess so."

"Do you want me to drive?"

"No. I'm fine." That was a slight exaggeration, but we weren't that far from his place.

Once in the car, I concentrated on driving. And the hard decision I had to make. Did I want to fight with him, or did I want to sleep with him?

Sex won.

We didn't fight until the next morning.

THREE

ON MONDAY, Natalie Thorson was arrested. Since she couldn't afford an attorney, the court appointed one.

Miriam Stern, who had once been part of the Public Defender's office and who still got some of the court-appointed overflow, called me just before noon. This was the second time she had been assigned a case in which I knew the defendant.

"Natalie wants to see you, and I'd like to talk to you, with her permission," Miriam said. She didn't identify herself, but the New York accent was unmistakable. "Right now, however, I want you to promise me that your only role in this will be as Natalie's therapist, a possible defense witness, and that you won't go running into the street after anybody who's carrying a gun."

"I have no intention of doing that ever again," I said. "And I wouldn't have done it the first time if I'd realized what a mess I was going to make of things."

"Good. Although you did help my client, in the midst of the mess. And I have to take partial responsibility, because I encouraged you to help him. So I'm not asking you to be hard on yourself. I'm only asking you to behave more prudently this time." Miriam paused long enough for the rebuke to sink in, then added, ''Natalie's in Sybil Brand until her mother can raise the money for the bail bond. If you want to stop by there this afternoon, I could see you on your way back, about four thirty.''

I normally reserved Sunday and Monday for days off, since I saw clients on Saturday, and a six-day week would be a quick trip to burnout, for me at least. Thus, I had no legitimate reason to refuse the request. I agreed to be at Miriam's office at four thirty.

The drive to Sybil Brand Institute, the women's jail, would have been fairly short from Silver Lake. From Sherman Oaks, it was a trek—Hollywood Freeway through heavy traffic to the downtown interchange, then the San Bernardino Freeway to the Ramona exit. Even in the middle of the day, the interchange was so clogged that I had more time than I wanted to think.

Especially I had to think when I passed Benson, the exit for Richard's apartment.

The argument Saturday morning had been serious. And it was over nothing, really. My stressed-out self-absorption versus his laid-back self-absorption. We each had a self image that involved personal growth and maturity, and looking back on where each of us had come from, there was an element of truth to it.

There was also an element of denial. Whatever the image, the inner child was alive and well. My inner child had managed to burst free of my outer adult long enough to say some things that his inner child didn't like. And now the question was whether I wanted to apologize. Or end the affair.

The trip wasn't long enough for me to decide.

Anyway, I had another demon to confront, besides the argument, namely, Miriam Stern's request that I behave more prudently. She was right, of course, that I hadn't behaved prudently, I had in fact behaved rashly, when I had been working to help another of her clients, a young man from that same block Richard lived on, who had been falsely accused of murder.

I wasn't happy about some of the consequences. I was even guilt-ridden, especially when I woke up in the middle of the night and wondered how much responsibility I bore for the death of my druggie ex-boyfriend. Knowing he had been committing slow suicide for years didn't help.

At the same time, I had enjoyed the rush of adrenaline that came with the danger. I had been engaged and excited when I talked to the drug dealer and looked for the real murderer in a way that I hadn't felt since I lost my *Coffee Time* job, a way I didn't feel when I was behaving prudently. There is a kick in doing live television, in performing without a net, and I had done it five mornings a week for five years. I hadn't realized how much I missed the adrenaline flow until I felt the rush of jeopardy in the street.

Of course, I had taken the thrill too far in my television days, when I discovered how much I could enhance the excitement with a little snort of cocaine before I went on the air. Just as I had taken the thrill too far when I tried to help my neighbor, Miriam Stern's client.

With luck, this time I wouldn't have to face a choice between behaving prudently or not.

The Ramona exit from the freeway finally presented itself. I was dumped at the bottom of a hill with a couple of ways to go. One led upward, to a golf course and two pretentious theme restaurants with gorgeous views. The other led around the hill to the jail. I drove around the hill.

The road followed along a chain-link fence to a turnout and a parking lot. A guardhouse sat blocking a gate.

I parked the Taurus in the lot and walked to the guardhouse.

A young man in a brown deputy's uniform smiled and nodded at me through the open top half of a double door.

"Faith Cassidy," I said.

He found my name on a clipboard and made a check beside it. Then he opened the bottom half of the door and let me in.

"You'll have to leave some form of picture ID here," he said. "You can pick it up on your way out."

I extracted my driver's license from my wallet and handed it to him. He slipped it into a plastic cover with a ring attached and dropped it onto one of many hooks on a corkboard.

"Do you know where you're going?" he asked.

"I'm a therapist, and one of my clients is in here," I told him. "She's expecting me, but I don't know where."

He pointed through an open door on the side of the guardhouse, to a path that led along a low building on one side, a yard on the other. On the far side of the yard was the main body of the Institute, five hulking stories of gray concrete.

"All the way to the end, then to your left," he said. "I'll phone ahead."

The yard held a chill that the January afternoon sun couldn't warm.

The low building held a collection of rooms with unbarred windows. I couldn't see much, but each one seemed to hold a group of women engaged in some kind of activity. One group seemed to be sewing. Another room held equipment for a small beauty parlor, where women in pink uniforms shampooed other women in pink uniforms.

A female deputy dressed just like the man at the guardhouse was waiting for me beside a heavy steel door that led into the big building.

I followed her a short distance into a dark hall, and then into a room that looked so familiar I had to remind myself I had only seen its duplicate on television, the one with the bright fluorescent lights where visitors sit on one side of the long table, inmates on the other, with glass in between them and phone receivers to talk through, and low barriers that didn't even offer the illusion of privacy in between each visitor. It was smaller and more cramped than it seemed on television.

I took a seat, and Natalie was ushered to the other side a moment later, wearing the same pink uniform I had seen on the women in the beauty parlor. She had only been there a few hours, and already she seemed to have that jailhouse pallor. Her hair looked as if it had been washed in lye.

"How are you doing?" I asked.

"Terrible. It's terrible." She leaned forward, speaking quietly. Tears welled over red-rimmed eyes and ran slowly down her cheeks. "They put me on a bus with women who smelled worse than anything I've ever smelled in my life, and we had to take disinfectant showers, and I'm in a dormitory cell more crowded than I could have imagined, barely space to move between the bunk beds. Please, please, tell them I didn't do it, please help me get out of here."

"I'll do what I can. I'm going to see Miriam Stern when I leave here," I said. "How much do you want me to say to her?"

"Anything. Everything," Natalie whispered. "She said she knows you. That's good. Maybe she'll believe you when you say I didn't kill Craig."

"Why did they decide to arrest you?" I asked.

"Fingerprints," Natalie's voice rose to a moan. "They found my fingerprints."

"On the knife?" I clenched my fist below the table.

"No, but in Craig's apartment. I'd been inside, but not that night." Natalie hesitated, then continued. "Except I guess someone saw my car, so the police knew I was lying about not having left my own house."

"Oh, Natalie," I said, shaking my head. "That's the trouble with lying to the cops. Once you do it, everything else you say is suspect."

"But I'm not lying to you," she said, leaning forward until her nose almost touched the glass. "I swear I didn't kill him."

"And I believe you." I had to believe her. Otherwise, my own guilt would be too much to bear. "Miriam Stern believes you, too, or she will after she and I have talked. Can you think of anyone else who might have wanted to kill Craig?"

"I'm trying," she moaned. "The cops asked me that, too. But I just didn't know that much about his life."

"Did he have a girlfriend? Business problems?" I asked.

"Jimmy saw Craig somewhere with a woman a couple of days before the murder, so maybe he had a girlfriend, but Jimmy said she looked like a hooker. And Craig always had business problems, I've told you that," she said.

"I don't remember right now," I said. "Tell me again."

When I first started seeing clients, I was embarrassed to admit that I didn't remember every last detail of their lives from session to session. Since then I've learned that it doesn't matter, because they enjoy telling the story a second time, especially if it involves dumping on an ex.

"Craig's a stockbroker, and he made a ton of money, but then he lost it all day-trading his own account," Natalie said, beginning to perk up at the thought of Craig going broke. "He was trying to find new clients—he'd lost most of his old ones—and he had to have been borrowing from somewhere to maintain his apartment and his car in the meantime, I don't know where. He must have clients who hate him, every stockbroker who loses big does. And whoever loaned him money could have gotten nervous. Do you think this was about money?''

''Well, maybe,'' I said. ''He was murdered in the kitchen, though, stabbed with his own kitchen knife, and that means he knew his killer pretty well. Money's a start, but there has to be more than that.''

''I'll keep thinking,'' Natalie said, nodding.

She was beginning to have a little color in her cheeks.

''Okay. And I hate mentioning this, but Natalie, I seem to remember something about bad investments costing you a lot of money, too. Right?'' The story was coming back from whatever brain file client stories get dumped in.

''Well, it depends on what you mean by a lot,'' she hedged.

''Enough to have destroyed any thought of community property, reduced you to borrowing money from your mother to supplement the child support you get from your first ex for Sarah, and caused you to seek out a therapist at a free clinic after you and Craig separated,'' I pointed out.

''Just until I could get past my depression and find a job,'' she argued. ''I really meant to find a job.''

''I know. Nobody would hire you because you were too depressed to come off well in an interview, and then you got more depressed,'' I said. ''But that's going to sound like motive to the police.''

''Who's side are you on, Faith?''

''Yours. You know that. I'm just trying to get a realistic idea of the situation.'' And right now, realistically, it wasn't terrific.

"Maybe the police will come up with another suspect," she said.

"Natalie, they think you did it. They aren't looking for anyone else."

Her face fell so far that I wished I hadn't said that.

"As I told you, I'm going to see Miriam Stern when I leave here," I continued. "The case against you is circumstantial, and she's a good attorney, and maybe we can figure out a way to make this disappear."

"Thanks, Faith. I'll never forget this, I promise, and when I get out of here and get a job, I'll find a way to pay you for your time. I mean that." Natalie looked at me through large, dark eyes, and I knew she did mean it. I hoped, for her sake more than mine, she could do it.

We exchanged good-byes, and the deputy came to return her to her cell.

I made my way back to the guardhouse, retrieved my driver's license, and left. The day seemed a little warmer as soon as I reached the parking lot, away from the shadow of the jail.

I drove back down the hill to civilization, which meant creeping along on the freeway the few miles to downtown L.A., then creeping along the surface streets to the old high rise that held Miriam Stern's office.

For the last several months I had managed to avoid going downtown, and thus experienced sticker shock at yet another raise in parking garage prices. This was going to be a short conversation.

The good thing about the parking garage was that

I could take an elevator straight up to the office, without having to set foot on the sidewalk. Downtown L.A. seemed to spite all efforts to turn it into a people-friendly city center. The sidewalks simply had weird vibes.

The reception area of the law firm hadn't changed from my last visit. The room still had the seedy look that comes from too many clients who need help they can't pay for, something I was going to have to watch out for in my own practice, I knew that. Even the plants seemed in the same stage of yielding to the despair of bound roots and insufficient water. I sat on the edge of a faded brown armchair, ignoring the tattered magazines on the scarred coffee table, waiting for Miriam to come get me.

She was only fifteen minutes late.

"Thanks for coming," she said, holding out a bony hand to shake mine, then leading me down the hall into the combination conference room and library.

Miriam had gained a little in authority from the first time I had seen her. I had thought then that she looked too young, too short, and too thin to be an attorney, but Ally McBeal had changed my mind about that, and at least Miriam Stern was sensible and organized. Frizzy black hair framed a small white face with piercing dark eyes devoid of makeup, and tiny arms peeked out from the rolled sleeves of a black jacket that hung shapelessly from her thin shoulders. She sat at one end of the table and opened a file. I slipped into the chair to her right.

"Natalie says you knew she wanted to kill her ex-husband." Miriam looked up at me, scowling, and waited for a reply.

"I knew she had a fantasy of killing Craig," I said. "I didn't think she was capable of carrying it out. And I don't think she killed him. I'm ready to say that in court."

"Are you ready for the civil suit from his family if she's convicted?" Miriam asked.

"Because I didn't report her fantasy? Come on. If I had believed she presented a danger to her ex, I would have reported it. I used some professional judgment here," I replied. "Besides, if I had reported her, and there was some kind of legal repercussion for her, and she wasn't serious about the threat, she could have sued me. How do I not get sued here?"

"You don't get sued if you made the right choice and if I get her off," Miriam said. "So far Natalie is refusing to even think about a plea bargain. We're going to have to hope for a sympathetic jury that doesn't like circumstantial evidence."

"So what can I do to help?"

"Be a credible witness when the time comes. Beyond that, nothing. I mean that. Nothing. Let me emphasize, *nothing.*" She softened it, though, with a quick flash of smile. "Except maybe, if you can, keep Natalie's spirits up. Depressed defendants don't go over well with juries." Miriam looked back at the file and scowled again. "I wish I could tell you I had something else, Faith, but I don't. Was she battered or anything?"

"Don't sound so hopeful. She wasn't battered, except the kind of psychological battery that comes from trusting someone with your life and then finding yourself broke and abandoned,'' I said.

"No law against broke and abandoned." Miriam sighed. "I'll have to think some more."

"Miriam, battered woman defense would only work if you thought she did it. Please tell me you don't think she did it," I begged.

"I don't know whether she did it. I wanted to meet with you because I wanted to be certain that you don't think she did it, that you aren't helping her just to cover your own credibility as a therapist," Miriam said calmly. "If you're going to be a defense witness, I have to know that your testimony will help the defense."

"If I thought she killed him, I'd throw myself on my sword," I said, looking her straight in the eye. "If I thought I had made such a serious error in professional judgment, I'd tear up my license."

There was enough truth in what I said that I could carry it off.

"Okay. I believe you." Miriam closed the file and stood up. "I'll be in touch."

She led the way out of the conference room and back to the front door of the firm. She held out her hand, and when I took it, I found myself looking her straight in the eye again, although I had to drop my head to do it.

"Behave prudently," she said. "Promise."

"Promise." I wished there were some way I could cross my fingers. I crossed them in my imagination. I had no business promising something I wasn't certain I could deliver.

I rode back down in the elevator, retrieved my car, and joined the slow procession out to the Valley on the Hollywood Freeway. By the time I reached my apartment, I was thoroughly depressed.

I ignored Amy and Mac, picked up the phone, and called Michael.

"My client has been arrested for her ex-husband's murder," I told him. "I have to prove she's innocent. And I don't know where to start."

FOUR

Of course Michael tried to talk me out of it.

"Anybody can get sued for anything, Faith, but in fact, I'd bet against anybody suing you over this murder," he argued. "For one thing, the jury will have to find your client guilty on circumstantial evidence. Nothing ties her directly to the crime. For another, I read somewhere that civil litigation peaked a few years ago and is now declining, with fewer people filing silly suits. And for still a third thing, you don't have any assets worth suing for."

His points were good ones.

And since he didn't think I should try to investigate, he made no suggestions on where to start.

But that didn't matter, because the answer came to me in the night. I woke up in the morning realizing that the clinic had to have some information on Natalie Thorson, including the address of the house where she and her children lived, and her son, Jimmy, was the one who had seen Craig with a woman. Since it was Tuesday, and I had to go to Silver Lake anyway, I could take a few minutes at the end of the afternoon to see if Jimmy was around.

Setting my own concerns aside so that I can deal with clients is easy some days, hard others. This was one of the hard days, especially since my last client of the afternoon was a twenty-year-old who could have solved all of her problems if she'd been willing to leave her abusive boyfriend, move in with her mother, take a menial job, and go back to school. I could understand why she didn't want to, but I still hoped she would do it. The hour dragged while I listened to her complaints, knowing nothing I said would make a difference.

Mary wasn't happy with the idea of giving me Natalie Thorson's address and telephone number without getting somebody's permission first.

"She would give it to me," I pleaded. "I didn't think to ask her while I was visiting her at the jail, and I don't want to go back there until I have to. But I need to talk to her son, I really do. I think it will help her defense. And you know she would want me to do anything that would help her defense."

"If anybody asks, you looked in the files while my back was turned," Mary said, writing the address and phone number on a slip from a message pad.

"Absolutely," I told her, dropping the piece of paper in my purse. That was a dangerous thing to do, in that I have a large, black leather bag, and pieces of paper have been known to slide to the bottom and never reappear. I hoped it would stay near the top until I could look at it with my glasses on. "I owe you a favor."

"I'll collect," Mary said, nodding.

Once in the car, I fished my glasses and the piece of paper out. Natalie lived a few blocks from where Richard did, but in an even worse neighborhood.

I drove the few blocks east on Sunset, turned right, then left to Natalie's street, and began to wonder if dropping in on Jimmy was a smart thing to do. This wasn't an area where strangers were welcome, and I was still committed to prudent behavior. Almost every one of the bungalows on the block needed paint. The others were built of weathered brick. Almost every one had bars on the windows and a metal fence around the yard.

The small house Natalie rented—chipped stucco that had once been white—was no exception. The gate was open, however, and so was the front door. A battered Honda was parked in the driveway of the detached garage.

I parked in front of the open gate, took a deep breath, and got out of the car.

"Hi, Jimmy," I called from the sidewalk. "Are you there?"

Nothing happened for a few seconds. Then a tall, thin, male figure wearing torn jeans and a faded T-shirt appeared in the doorway. The long white face and the limp dark hair marked him unmistakably as Natalie's son.

"Who are you?"

"I'm your mother's friend," I said. "Could I talk to you?"

He laughed and shook his head.

"I didn't think my mother had any friends. And she's in jail, if you want to talk to her."

"I know she's in jail. I visited her yesterday." I walked through the gate, along the sidewalk as far as the steps to the porch, and held out my hand. "I'm Faith Cassidy."

"Oh, right." He came down the steps to meet me. His handshake was as limp as his hair. "You're the shrink from the clinic. Can you get her out of jail?"

"No, I'm afraid not. Or not right away, anyway. I understand that your grandmother is raising money for the bail bond. She'll be out then."

He shrugged his shoulders. "Grandma doesn't have any money either. She hasn't been able to help us much before, and I know she's scared of losing her house. I don't know where she's going to come up with something for a bail bond. So I guess Mom has to stay in jail for a while. If you want to know what I think, I don't think Mom killed Craig. But I wouldn't have blamed her if she had."

"Are you saying your grandmother lost money through Craig's advice, too?" I tried to remember whether Natalie had mentioned that.

"Not a lot, I guess, compared with what Mom lost. But Grandma didn't have a lot to lose," he answered.

"And why wouldn't you have blamed your mother if she had killed Craig? Just because of the lost money?"

"Who's she, Jimmy?"

The question came before Jimmy could answer mine.

A young woman Jimmy's height, but a couple of years older and about thirty pounds heavier, came out of the house. She had curly black hair and olive skin, and her T-shirt and jeans were in better shape than his. When she joined us, she slipped two possessive arms around his waist.

"She's my mom's shrink," Jimmy said. "Faith Cassidy, Alicia Hernandez."

"Yeah? She gonna help your mom?" Alicia regarded me skeptically.

"I hope so," I said. I didn't bother holding out my hand, since Alicia hadn't made one of hers available.

"Then you oughta talk to her, Jimmy," Alicia said. "Your mom needs all the help she can get."

"Come on in the house," Jimmy said.

I followed him up to the porch and through the open front door.

The room was small and dark, with brocade drapes half-drawn against the afternoon sun, and the furniture was too big, clearly having been bought for another space. Two armchairs and a sofa with dark brocade upholstery were crowded against a mahogany coffee table. A glass-topped wrought iron table that should have graced a patio held a small television set. The pieces were crammed so tightly together that there was barely room to walk. A heavy ceramic vase in the corner held a bouquet of dead chrysanthemums.

Everything was coated with the fine dust of old dreams. Just walking into the room would have sent a healthy person into a funk. Natalie should have sold the furniture and started over.

"You want coffee?" Alicia asked.

"No, thank you," I replied.

"Okay. Have a seat." She worked her way around the coffee table to the sofa. Jimmy followed her, and

I took one of the chairs. "So what do you wanna know?"

I really wanted to know whether Alicia had moved in, and if she had, whether Natalie knew, but that wasn't why I had come. With luck, one of them would volunteer that information.

"I want to see if I can come up with some names of people other than Natalie who might have wanted Craig dead," I said. "The police aren't trying to find anyone else, and I thought it might help her attorney, if she knew there were other possible suspects. And I also want to know why you wouldn't have blamed your mother for killing him."

Alicia turned expectantly to Jimmy.

"My stepfather was a son-of-a-bitch," Jimmy said. "I will never figure out why Mom married him. Lots of people besides Mom must have wanted him dead."

As I remembered it, Natalie had married Craig because he was great in bed and spent money wildly. I didn't volunteer the information.

"In what way was he a son-of-a-bitch?" I asked.

"He smiled at people to their faces and said mean things behind their backs. All he wanted was their money," Jimmy answered.

"Even if lots of people wanted him dead, the fact that he was stabbed in his kitchen sounds more like a crime of passion than anything else," I said. "If money was involved, it had to be on top of some other passion. Natalie told me you saw Craig with another woman. When was it and where were they? Can you tell me anything about her?"

"They were coming out of a bar on Wilshire Boulevard, Halloran's," he said. "Not Beverly Hills, but on the way. It's downstairs from the stockbroker office where Craig worked. She was a lot younger than him. Lots of dark hair, short leather skirt, she looked like a hooker. It was only like six o'clock on a weeknight, though, I'm not sure which day, so maybe he met her after work or something. And it was just a couple of nights before he was killed."

"Was that his style?" I only knew Craig from Natalie's description, and I would have expected a little more class.

Jimmy shrugged. "Drinking after work? Yeah. Making it with hookers? Who knows? Other than that one time, I never saw him with anybody but Mom."

"What else can you tell me about her?"

"Nothing. She had light brown skin, like half of L.A., and I wasn't close enough to see anything more."

"Did you know any of his male friends?"

"What friends? He and Mom used to entertain a lot, but then the financial thing happened, and nobody wanted to know them." Jimmy crossed his arms defensively.

Alicia leaped in.

"Tell her about the guy," she said.

Jimmy glared. I waited.

"Craig had an argument with some dude in a Porsche, right before he moved out," Jimmy said. "Where we used to live. The dude wouldn't get out of his car, so I didn't get a good look at him, and Craig looked white as death after the dude drove away. I asked Mom about it, but she wouldn't talk."

"That was several months ago," I pointed out.

"Yeah. But suppose it was more than money," Alicia said. "Suppose Craig got it on with the guy's wife or something, and suppose he didn't stop doing her when the guy found out. Maybe it just took a long time for the guy to do something."

"Okay, I'll ask Natalie about the guy and the argument the next time I see her," I said. "In the meantime, maybe you could write down Craig's address for me, and the address of this bar on Wilshire, Halloran's, where you saw him with the woman."

I pulled a small notepad and a pen out of my bag and handed them to Jimmy. He scribbled the addresses and handed them back.

"I'm glad somebody's helping Mom," he said.

"Do you have a picture of Craig?" I asked.

He frowned. "Mom had some of the two of them. Hang on while I look."

He left me alone with Alicia.

"You need any help at that clinic place?" she asked. "I'm looking for work. So is Jimmy. We gotta pay the rent on this house for a while. Until his mom gets out of jail, anyway."

I was certain Natalie would be thrilled to hear that her arrest had shaken Jimmy out of his commitment to unemployment. I hoped it would last long enough for him to actually find a job.

"The clinic doesn't have many paid employees," I said. She gave me a half-smile to let me know that was the kind of answer she had been expecting. "What skills do you have?"

"I played volleyball in high school."

"Is that your way of telling me that you weren't much of a student?"

"I did okay. But nothing I learned helped me get a job. Or Jimmy either."

"And neither one of you went on to college," I pointed out.

"So what are you telling me?" she asked.

"You'll have to look for a job where they're willing to train you. And none of those jobs pay very well to start," I answered. "With both of you working, you may be able to make the rent, though."

"Great," she said. "I hope you do a better job of helping Jimmy's mom."

I bit my tongue to keep from launching into a lecture on personal responsibility that wouldn't have done either of us any good. Fortunately, Jimmy came back before I had to think of anything else to say.

"I found a wedding picture," he said.

He handed me one of those soft gray cardboard folders that open to reveal a framed photograph.

The picture showed a Natalie that I only could have imagined, a laughing Natalie, with color in her cheeks and bounce in her hair, wearing a light blue dress and holding a bouquet of white carnations and purple iris.

The man with her was good-looking in a sort of aging roué way, especially his open smile and his wavy salt-and-pepper hair. But he had the heavy jowls and florid complexion of someone who ate and drank too much. He hadn't even bothered to put down his champagne flute for the photo.

He was also several inches taller and many pounds

heavier than Natalie. I tried to imagine her with the courage to come at him with a knife. I couldn't.

"Thanks," I said. I hesitated before asking the next question, but decided to go for it. "I don't suppose your father could help out with the bail bond. Or what do you think?"

One more shoulder shrug. I would have been a lousy mother. The shoulder shrugs alone would have made me crazy.

"Maybe if Sarah got in touch with him, maybe he'd help Sarah. He tries to get custody of Sarah every once in a while. Mom thinks it's just so he won't have to pay child support, but I think he cares about Sarah. He won't help me unless I go to college, though, and he'd let Mom rot in jail before he'd lift a finger to help her." Jimmy said it with the same lack of affect that had characterized Natalie's depression.

I decided not to pursue that issue. I dropped both the notepad with the addresses and the photograph into my bag and fished out a business card.

"Thanks again for your help," I said, handing him the card. "Call me if you think of anything that might help me get your mother out of trouble."

Alicia took the business card out of his hand.

"Sure," she said. "Thanks for taking the trouble to stop by."

We all stood up. Neither one of them walked me out.

I knew the bar was a long shot, unless Craig stopped in regularly, but the only way to find out was to go there. Since Jimmy saw Craig at the bar on a weeknight, Tuesday was probably as good a time as any. And I was going to hit such miserable traffic going back to the Valley that I wasn't in any hurry to begin.

So I decided to do one more thing as long as I was in Silver Lake, before I checked the bar. I decided to apologize to Richard.

Not that I believed any of the things I said when we were fighting were inaccurate. Unfortunately, I was right on, and it's the true things that hurt. Thus, it was up to me to show some maturity, take the first step to make up, demonstrate that the inner child can be nurtured without being allowed to run the whole show.

I dropped back to Sunset, drove the few blocks to Coronado, then took a couple of twists and turns south to Richard's apartment.

As I parked the car, as I walked along the drive, as I walked up the stairs to his apartment, I rehearsed the words, truly prepared to be generous.

My first knock got no response.

His Harley was there, though, in his parking spot, and I figured his mind was wrapped up in his work.

So I knocked a little louder, and I called out, "Richard, it's me, Faith!"

Still silence.

I was about to knock a third time when he answered the door in his blue terrycloth bathrobe, face flushed.

"Faith, listen, this isn't a good time," he said.

Before I could ask why, a voice from behind him said, "Oh, just tell her."

Cydnee, wearing nothing but multiple earrings and thong underpants, grabbed his arm and smiled. Or smirked, really. She was young, thin, almost naked, smirking, and holding on to the arm of someone who said he loved me and wanted to live with me.

"Oops," I said, managing to smile in return. I wiggled a good-bye with my fingers, turned, and walked down the steps without looking back.

"Faith, damn it, I'm sorry," Richard yelled. "I'll call you tonight."

I wanted to do something, say something in response, but all I could do was keep walking. I got in the car, started it, and drove away on automatic pilot. As soon as I got around the corner, I parked it again.

My inner child needed to cry.

FIVE

IN TRUTH, I would have felt worse, or at least given in to self-pity more, if I hadn't planned on going to the bar, if I hadn't had a task to accomplish, a client who needed my help.

But I did, and I wanted to keep moving, so I managed to pull myself together, redo my makeup, and refocus my energy. I even ended up feeling a little proud of myself for doing it.

More than that, I could now feel justified in refusing to live with Richard. Suppose that had been our apartment, not his?

"Lucky you found out while you had your own place," I said to myself, aloud, because I needed to hear myself say it. My voice was firm.

I started the car and began to pull out into the street. A blaring horn stopped me, and I realized I hadn't checked for traffic.

"Pay attention to your driving," I said, also aloud. "An accident won't help the situation."

That one I actually believed.

I managed to drive to the bar and park the car in an outrageously expensive garage without inciting anyone's road rage.

When I saw the place, I became a little more optimistic at the thought that someone might know Craig, if not the woman who had been with him. Halloran's was a pseudo-Irish pub on the ground floor of a financial services high rise, the kind of place where a lot of stockbrokers who worked upstairs might hang out.

The inside was dark, with fake wood paneling, lit almost entirely by neon signs advertising various brands of beer and whiskey. The noise level was my first clue that a surprising number of tables were occupied by cheerful men who sounded as if they had been there awhile, surprising because it wasn't quite five o'clock. I wondered if the place was that busy every afternoon.

I found a seat at the bar between two men who were each engaged in heavy conversation with someone sitting on the other side, got the wedding photograph out of my purse, and waited for the bartender to come to me.

Instead of asking for an order, he slammed both hands on the bar in front of me and nodded, without smiling. He was round-faced and balding, wearing a striped shirt with the sleeves rolled up, and he looked as if he could double as a bouncer if necessary.

"White wine," I said, flustered by his brisk approach.

"House wine or something a little better?" he asked.

"Something a little better," I said.

He nodded again, as if that was the right response, and he had a too-full glass in front of me almost before I could open the photo folder.

"I'm looking for information about this man," I said.

"Then look in this morning's paper," he answered. "Craig Thorson, murdered a few nights ago. Got his ex-wife in jail for it. That's her right next to him in the picture."

"Then you do know him?" I asked.

"He's been in a few times." He started to turn away.

"With whom?" I asked quickly.

The bartender stopped, puzzled. Then he chuckled.

"First time I heard the word 'whom' in this bar. You spent too many years in graduate school, honey. Why do you want to know about Craig?"

"I'm helping his ex-wife's attorney get information about the case," I said, figuring that was close enough to the truth. I ignored the remark about graduate school. He was right, but it was none of his business. "We believe Natalie Thorson is innocent. Craig Thorson was seen leaving this bar with a woman a few days before his murder. We want to find that woman."

"Yo, Bill, how about some service?" someone called from the other end of the bar.

"Be with you in a second," the bartender called back. He added, to me, "Guys are in and out of here with women all the time. Sorry I can't help you."

"Thanks anyway," I said to the back of his bald head. He was already taking care of the next customer.

I took a sip of the wine—better than I expected—

and looked around, trying to decide which of the many drinkers might have known Craig.

The man sitting on my right, momentarily alone, turned to me and smiled.

I flipped open the photograph.

"Know him?" I asked.

The man shook his head.

"I'm not a regular," he said. "You probably want to talk to Debbie. She'll be here at five."

"Thanks," I said, this time meaning it.

I was saved from further conversation when his friend returned from the restroom.

Among the glowing wall signs was a clock, one of those strange ones without numbers, just black dots glued to a mirror and the two hands moving around, the next thing to no clock at all. I couldn't conceive of trying to tell the time from it after a couple of drinks. The little hand was pointing at the dot to the right of the bottom one, and the big hand was almost straight up. I figured Debbie was due in about five minutes.

I hoped I didn't have to wait too long. The crowd was mostly male, mostly dressed in three-piece suits with loosened ties and unbuttoned shirt collars, and I wanted to be out of there before somebody besides the guy to my right decided I was alone, and thus available.

Unfortunately, somebody had already decided that.

A rosy-cheeked man with a full head of white hair, wearing the requisite three-piece, navy blue suit, leaned past my shoulder and put his hand on the bar.

"There's more room at the table," he said. His breath smelled of gin. "Why don't you join us?"

"Only if you can give me information about this man," I said, opening the wedding photo. "Otherwise, I'm waiting here for Debbie."

"You're asking about Craig?" The man laughed, a sharp sound that was almost a bark. "Debbie'll give you an earful, I'm sure. Why're you asking about Craig?"

"I'm looking for information that may help to clear his ex-wife of the murder charge," I said.

The man frowned and shook his head. "The police think it's the ex. They're usually right about that kind of thing. Are you a private detective or something?"

"No, I'm—"

He cut me off. "You look familiar. Haven't I met you somewhere? I'm Gary Parkman."

"I'm Faith Cassidy, and I don't think we've met."

"Wait, wait, wait a minute. Fay Cassidy, you used to do that show on television, I remember now." His rosy cheeks showed dimples when he smiled, and his slightly unfocused blue eyes lit up. He was almost cute. Not quite. That was one of the problems of having done morning television. People remembered seeing me in their own living rooms—or worse, in their bedrooms—and thought I was an old friend.

But I had to admit relief that, if he was going to remember me, he remembered me from television. Better that than the other possibility, that I had met him during a rough period in my life, one with a lot of memory gaps. I managed to smile back.

"Yes, but it's Faith, not Fay, and I haven't been

on television in a long time. I'm working with Natalie Thorson's attorney," I said.

"Come on," he said, hand now on my shoulder. "Jason said you were an actress. He'll be pleased to know he was right."

I would have argued, but I spotted a woman in jeans and sweater with a tray of drinks, probably Debbie, and I wanted to make contact. So I smiled, picked up my wine glass, and said, "Which table?"

Gary backed away far enough so that I could get up from the bar stool. The hand left my shoulder, then returned, guiding me toward a round table where five men were watching our progress.

I started to shift in Debbie's direction, but Gary's heavy hand stopped me.

"She'll be over," he said.

"Good work, Gary," one of the men at the table said, just a little too loudly.

Gary was the oldest of the six men. The one who called out looked middle-aged, the other four were thirty-something. The younger men, with their sleek dark hair and tailored dark suits, had that same expensively cloned look that always puzzled me in large talent agencies, in that I've never understood why men who were obviously bright and ambitious would all choose to look alike.

I missed their names in the noise, except for Jason, the middle-aged one, who high-fived Gary for bringing me to the table.

"Debbie, another round," Jason called out, "and one for the lady."

I was going to stop him, because I hadn't finished

my first glass, and I didn't want to stay for a second, but I did want to talk to Debbie. So I sat and smiled at them, one by one around the table.

"Fay is asking about Craig Thorson," Gary told them. "She's a private investigator, working with the ex-wife's attorney."

I should have corrected him, about the name and the occupation. I let it slide.

The five men immediately stopped smiling.

"Thank God it was a crime of passion," one of them said.

"What do you mean?" I asked.

"If it had been a disgruntled client, odds are he would have mowed down half the office with an Uzi," another one answered. "We've all been doing a lot of handholding these days."

"Handholding?"

"People who lose money blame the stockbroker," Jason said. "Want us to do something about it. Hell, nothing we can do. We don't want people to lose money—in a perfect world, everybody would have a ton of it—and God knows we have losses of our own. We didn't just recommend those stocks to other people, you know. The only thing you can do when somebody calls crying about losses is hold their hand until they feel better."

"Did you work with Craig?" I asked.

"No, just knew him from the bar here. But it's been the same for everybody," he answered. "Investors who've been in the market for a long time can weather the changes. But the long bull market and the dot-com fever brought in the people who used to keep their money in the mattress. Some of them have been pretty upset.''

''Well, okay. But does that necessarily mean Craig Thorson's death was a crime of passion?'' I asked.

''They got the ex-wife,'' Jason said. ''That's good enough for me.''

''And even if it is a crime of passion, does it have to be Natalie?'' I asked. ''I understand Craig was seen in here not long before his death with another woman.''

A ripple of chuckles passed from one man to the next.

''You're a great detective, honey,'' Gary said. ''Now you just have to find them.''

''Them?''

Before anyone could answer, Debbie slipped in next to Jason and began swiftly replacing empty glasses with full ones. She had the lean, hungry look of the aspiring actress, I knew it well. With the total confidence of youth and great cheekbones, she had pulled her long, lustrous, brown hair into a tight pony tail and shunned makeup.

I was glad I didn't have to diet for the camera anymore. Really. I could even argue that I looked a lot healthier with the added twenty pounds. Still, I felt a twinge of jealousy, not for her boniness, but for the hope that propelled it.

Somebody had to make it big. Maybe Debbie would.

''Debbie, this is Fay Cassidy. You might remember her, she used to be an actress,'' Gary said. ''She wants to ask you about Craig.''

Debbie wavered only for a moment.

"No time right now," she said.

"I only need a few minutes. When do you have a break?" I asked.

"Not for two hours, sorry."

"I still have a few Industry contacts." I took a shot.

And it stopped her.

"You got a card?" she asked.

I pulled out my card case and tried to hand her one, but Jason intercepted it with a leer.

All of a sudden half a dozen card cases were out, and within thirty seconds everyone had my card and I had each of theirs. I did manage to get one to Debbie, but only with effort.

"I'll call you tomorrow," she said, just before tearing off to the next table.

If she did, I was going to have to come up with somebody in the Industry who might still remember my name and take my call. If she didn't, I was off the hook, and I could come back another night, catch her closer to her break. In either case, she was a more likely source of useful information about Craig Thorson than my would-be drinking buddies. I finished my glass of wine—the first one—and stood.

"Gentlemen, it's been a pleasure meeting you," I said.

"You can't leave," Gary said, grabbing my hand. "We just bought you a drink. We'll be insulted."

His smile denied the words.

"And I appreciate the gesture, but I have to be somewhere else." Amy and Mac had to be fed. Actually, I had to be fed. That one glass of wine, on top of the stress of the day, had gone straight to my head. And I discovered when I stood up that I didn't have a lot of energy left.

I tried to extricate my hand, but Gary held on.

"I'll only let you go if you promise a rain check," he said.

"I promise." I could deal with that another time.

I squeezed his hand and managed to get mine loose.

There was some sort of general grumbling, but I smiled and waved at everyone, and made it to the door. I needed fresh air.

As soon as I was outside, I realized that I was looking at a drive to the Valley smack in the middle of rush hour. And there was no reason I couldn't have eaten something in the bar, except that I wanted to get away from that table full of faux cheer.

The block was all high-rise office buildings, and there didn't appear to be a restaurant where I could dash in and get something fast to go, something I could eat in the car. I knew that lobbies of these building held small convenience stores, but the idea of a cheese sandwich on white bread left over from the day before made even going back in the bar sound attractive.

I walked to the corner and spotted a deli a few doors away. Saved. I felt as if I had just been rescued from a shipwreck. I wanted to run, but contained myself. I half-jogged to the deli, glanced at the brief take-out menu, and ordered a sandwich.

The egg salad on whole wheat with a dill pickle on the side tasted better than any sandwich I could remember. I ate half of it standing in front of the counter.

"Are you okay?" asked the man who had made it for me.

"Fine, thank you," I said between bites.

I put the other half back in the brown bag to save for the ride home.

That ride took me almost an hour, on clogged freeways, and I thought again about moving somewhere closer to the clinic.

And that led to thinking about Richard. I didn't want to think about Richard, so I sang along with the car radio until I got home. I kept singing to myself as I fed the cats, and finally checked my answering machine.

The message from Richard said, "I'm sorry. It was a mistake. Please call me."

Instead, I poured myself a glass of wine and fixed a salad to go with it. The sandwich hadn't been quite enough for dinner, but I didn't want much more.

The phone rang while I was eating, and I listened while the machine took another message from Richard.

I returned the other messages, the ones from clients. About Richard—well, I had to sleep on it. I could call him back in the morning.

SIX

WHEN THE PHONE RANG in the morning, I answered before I remembered that letting the machine screen the calls might be a good idea unless I was ready to talk with Richard.

Ready or not, there he was.

"I'm sorry. I didn't mean to hurt you," he said. "I don't know what else to say. Help me out here."

"What if I'd been living with you?" I blurted.

"It wouldn't have happened." He said it so calmly, so confidently, I wanted to believe him. "You want it both ways, Faith. You want to be able to fight with me and walk out on me, have your own place to go to, but then you want me available—want my apartment available—if you decide to come back. I've offered commitment, you've turned it down, and now you're hurt because you don't have it."

"It's too early in the morning for me to handle that much accusation," I said. "It may be the truth. I'm not sure. I hadn't exactly turned down commitment, I just hadn't accepted it."

His silence let me know that he wasn't buying that one.

"I came over yesterday to apologize," I added. "I was going to tell you I was sorry about the fight."

"Okay. I'm sorry about it, too. What do you want to do now?"

"I want to know how it happened. How did you end up naked with Cydnee?"

"Well, I know this will sound lame, but she wanted me, and I just didn't see any reason to say no."

"You're right, Richard. It sounds lame."

"And all I can say is that I'm sorry. I didn't mean to hurt you. I love you, Faith. I want to live happily ever after with you. I'm just not sure that's possible," he said.

"I wish I believed in fairy tales." I waited for a response, but I didn't get one.

"All right, here's what I want to do. Let's give it a couple of days, each nurse our own wounds, and have dinner Friday." I said it bravely, but I closed my eyes to shield myself if he said no.

"Saturday," he said. "Can we make it Saturday?"

I bit my lip to keep from asking why. "Sure."

That settled, we had nothing more to say.

After I replaced the phone, I sat there and stared at it, daring it to ring again, knowing if he called back, I'd remind him that he was the one who had been in bed with someone else, and he had no right to shift guilt for it to me. The full measure of how upset I was hit me when Amy came over and nudged my leg, something she rarely did. I picked her up, and she promptly began to lick my face and purr. The last time she had done that, I had been so sick with the flu that I could barely move from dehydration. Mac hopped up on my knees, scrambling for balance, and my lap was suddenly crowded.

They did, however, manage to make me feel better. When the phone rang again a few minutes later, they hopped down, mission accomplished.

"What do you want to know about Craig Thorson?" Debbie asked.

"I want to know who, other than his ex-wife, had a motive to stab him to death," I replied. "The boys in the bar indicated that there were a lot of women in his life, and that you might be able to help me find some of them."

"Define 'some.'"

"I don't even know what 'a lot' is. I went in there because his ex-wife's son saw him coming out of that bar a few days before he was murdered with a woman who looked like a hooker. Do you remember her?" I asked.

"Oh, yes. He didn't just leave with her. He brought her in. He introduced her to everyone as Tory, but I didn't hear a last name. If that's even her real first name." The bitterness in her voice was too strong to be impersonal.

"Why do you dislike him so much?"

"Because I ended up in bed with him, of course, just like all the others did. What kind of therapist are you, anyway?"

Okay, I should have picked up on it. But I was still preoccupied with Richard.

"I would have thought he was a little too old for you," I said in my own defense. "And a little too alcoholic."

"He caught me in a weak moment," Debbie said. "And then did the wink, wink, nudge, nudge routine with his buddies the next night. I thought about killing him, but I didn't.''

''And I suppose you were working the night somebody else did.''

''Fortunately, I was, from five until midnight.''

''So do you know how I can get in touch with Tory?''

''Not unless you want to hang out on the corner of Sunset and La Brea waiting for her to show up.''

''Seriously?'' I couldn't tell from her voice.

''Or some other corner.'' Debbie sighed as if she were giving up on me. ''She's a pro, and I'm sure he paid her. Why aren't you looking at Craig's clients? You don't think his clients had motive?''

''Everything points to a crime of passion,'' I said.

''And you don't think he was screwing his female clients?''

That was so obvious once she said it that I had to cover.

''But that's still women he's screwing,'' I argued. ''And, one more time, can you help me find any of them?''

''No. I would see him with women sometimes, but he never introduced us. I'll keep my ears open, that's all I can promise. Those guys talk so much, and they're all after Craig's former clients, especially the ones he was screwing, so one of them is sure to drop a name.''

''Would one of them know why someone like Craig might pay a hooker?'' I asked. ''It sounds as if he could get whatever he wanted for free.''

''I think there was some kind of game, maybe a

bet, some kind of joke involved. You'll have to find out for yourself what it was. Now. Your turn." She paused for emphasis. "Was that a line about Industry contacts or are you really going to help me?"

"A little of both," I admitted. "Do you have an agent?"

"Not one I wouldn't say good-bye to in a New York minute," Debbie answered.

"Sam Melman was mine, and he hasn't heard from me in so long that he might return my call out of curiosity. Do you want to meet him?"

"If you can set it up, sure." She sounded skeptical, and I didn't blame her.

"Okay. What can I tell him about you?"

Her answer was nothing but acting classes and amateur theater, nothing I could use to interest Sam, who was one of the last of the influential independent agents, one of the last Patagonian toothfish who hadn't been swallowed by a whale.

"What do you think?" she asked.

"I'll do my best. Give me your telephone number."

She gave me her number, followed by her assurance that she would eavesdrop until she found a name of someone with a motive to murder Craig Thorson.

I reiterated the promise to do my best with Sam and hung up. Before I lost my nerve, I called Sam's office. He was, of course, on another line. I left a message with his secretary.

"Nothing important," I told her. "Whenever he isn't busy."

I wanted another latte before I decided what to do next. I was still steaming milk when the phone rang.

"What's that noise?" Sam asked in lieu of saying hello.

"The espresso machine. Hi."

"Hi. If you want to go back to work, Fay, I don't think I can help you."

"I'm not an actress anymore. I'm working as a therapist now, Sam. I went to graduate school, remember?" I didn't give him time to answer. "But I haven't forgotten you. And last night I met a young actress with the greatest cheekbones since Hepburn, either Hepburn, and I promised her I'd try to set up a meeting."

"Fay, honey, I have more clients than I can handle now. I'm not taking any new clients. So you're a therapist? No more drugs? If you want to write a book about your recovery, I can put you in touch with somebody. But you'd have to name names from your weird period," he said.

"It wasn't that weird," I began, and although that was the truth, I knew that anything I said to Sam would sound like rationalization. If I heard someone say she wasn't an addict, just a user, and if I knew she blew her television career through an accusation of unreliability, no matter how unjust, I wouldn't believe her, either. "Thanks for the thought, but no thanks. Really, I just want to do this woman—and you—a favor by getting you together."

"Not me. But I brought somebody into the office, just for cases like this where I don't want to say no. You want to do this girl a favor, I want to do you a favor, tell her she can see my new associate, David Jacobson. Okay?'' He was ready to get off the phone, I could tell. Probably someone more important on another line.

"Okay. I'll tell her to call David Jacobson. Her name is Debbie," I said, realizing that I had neglected to ask for her last name.

"Terrific. Debbie. I'll tell David, a Debbie with cheekbones. And let me know if you want to write a book.''

"I don't think so."

"Don't say never. You may want some money sometime. We'll do lunch.''

That was Sam's way of saying good-bye.

I dutifully called Debbie back and gave her the sort of good news.

"Yeah, well, Sam Melman's associate is better than what I've got," she said. "Thanks. I'll call you.''

At least she didn't suggest we do lunch.

I called Michael so I would have someone to commiserate with me while I drank my latte.

"Where do I start?" he exclaimed, when I had brought him up to date on the events of the last two days.

"With Richard. He had no right to make me feel guilty when he went to bed with that young, thin artist.''

"No, of course not, except that you already felt guilty about not committing and you didn't have to feel any guiltier if you didn't want to," he said. "If it were me, and I wanted the relationship, I'd give him this one. But it's you. Do you want the relationship? Or do you just want to be the one who leaves, not the one who is left?"

"I just don't know."

"Well, call me Sunday morning and tell me how you behaved Saturday night. That ought to give us a clue. Now, about the perils of Natalie Thorson." He made it sound like the title of a soap opera. I could see his point. "Are you sure this is a good idea?"

"I told you, I don't want to get sued by Craig Thorson's family. And all I've done is ask Debbie to eavesdrop on Craig's buddies. That's not dangerous," I argued.

"Why am I the only one who can visualize the dangers in confronting a murderer?" Michael asked. "The only one who thinks a lawsuit isn't a fate worse than death? Who are these terrifying members of Craig Thorson's family?"

"You've just taken a huge leap here. I'm not confronting a murderer. All I'm doing is finding out who might have a motive."

"Okay. Right. And you'll let me know if you contemplate something more?"

That I could safely agree to.

I didn't feel as much better when I got off the phone as I had hoped. I wanted Michael to say something that would make me feel better about Cydnee and Debbie, both young and gorgeous and sleeping with out-of-bounds men as if sex were as safe as it used to be. But I hadn't told him I was envious, so he hadn't told me I didn't need to be. I would have to conquer that demon on my own.

I took my latte out to the patio and sat on the chaise, looking out into the sunshine and the greenery. What was my next step? Should I just wait for Debbie to get back to me? Even as I thought it, I knew I wasn't going to wait. Gary Parkman was clearly part of the same old-boy cohort as Craig Thorson, and there was a possibility that he would be more forthcoming away from the others.

The day was too pleasant to mess it up immediately. I waited until I finished my latte before I called Gary Parkman.

And I needed to think about the other question Michael had raised, namely, who were these members of Craig Thorson's family? The ones who might sue me. The ones who might also have motives for murder. I would have to ask Natalie, and that would mean another trip to Sybil Brand, unless Miriam had been able to bail her out, and surely one of them would have called me if she had.

But not today. I couldn't face the freeways, especially since I had three clients coming to the apartment that afternoon. Seeing Natalie could wait.

I called the number on Gary Parkman's business card, expecting either a secretary or a voice mail message, and was surprised that he answered his own phone.

"Hey, Fay, great to hear from you," he said. "I was going to call you. Do I get the rain check for the drink?"

"Absolutely. How about Friday evening?" I felt a slight twinge as I said it, but this wasn't a date.

"We'll do it. Seven o'clock. Where do you live? I'll pick you up."

"No, we can meet. No sense in you driving all the way out here," I said firmly.

"You're sure you want to drive over here?" he asked.

"I'm sure." If he came to me, he might think it was a date.

He picked a restaurant on the Westside that had been around long enough to have survived being trendy and settled in with a reputation for good food and service. I agreed, and that was the end of the conversation.

And before I put down the phone, I called Miriam Stern's office for an update.

This time I got voice mail.

Having done all I could on that front, I turned my attention to my clients.

Fortunately, none of the ones scheduled for the afternoon had demanding problems, and I was still feeling pretty good when I got around to checking my answering machine. Miriam Stern's message said that yes, Natalie was still in jail because no, her mother hadn't been able to come up with bail.

Natalie's regularly scheduled appointment with me would have been the next morning at ten. It made sense to keep that appointment, then, at Sybil Brand.

Going there the second time was no easier than going the first time. I tried to imagine what it would feel like to walk through that gate without knowing when you would come out. And then I tried to forget what I imagined.

Natalie seemed a little less distraught than when I had seen her three days before. I hoped that was positive, not a sign that she was sinking back into her depression. Her eyes were dull, though, and she had trouble keeping them focused.

"How are you feeling?" I asked.

"I don't know, Faith," she said, shaking her head. "I think I may have to shut down feeling. There's too much feeling in here."

"Don't shut down. This won't last forever. I'm sure your mother is doing her best to get the bail money together," I said.

"But what if she can't?" The words were barely more than a whisper.

"Then you have to hang in until I find out something that will help."

That penetrated.

"Do you think you can find out who killed Craig?" Natalie asked, suddenly alert.

"I don't know, but maybe I can at least come up with some suspects. Evidently more than one woman was mad at him, and he may have been screwing his clients literally as well as figuratively. I just don't have anything concrete," I told her.

"Jimmy said you stopped by to see him, that you were asking questions about the woman he saw with Craig. Did you find out who she is?"

"Not exactly. I'm working on it. Have you thought of anything that might help?"

"No." The light went out of her eyes.

"What about family members? Are there any members of Craig's family who might have been mad at him?'' I felt a little guilty about getting what I needed to know this way, but not so guilty that I didn't do it.

"He only has a sister. His parents are dead, and he didn't have children by either of his former wives."

"Former wives? Has anyone checked with his former wives?" I asked.

"Well, one is remarried and living in Cincinnati, and the other moved to Ojai to concentrate on her spiritual growth, so I don't think either one is too likely to have murdered him," Natalie said. "I don't know about his sister."

"Tell me about her."

"She's on some kind of disability, and he was supporting her. I didn't spend much time with her, because she always seemed so spaced out, as if she were on heavy meds or something."

"Give me a name and address," I said, pulling my notebook out of my bag.

"Julie Thorson. She lives in the Valley, in one of those big condo complexes north of the Simi Freeway, and I don't remember the exact address. Jimmy can find it for you, if she isn't listed in the phone book."

"Okay, I'll talk to her. And one more thing. Jimmy said that Craig had an argument with a man in a Porsche, while you still lived in the old house, an argument that left Craig white. Do you remember anything about it?"

Natalie frowned, as if old-house memories were not something she wanted to revisit.

"Not off the top of my head," she answered. "I'll try to think of somebody who drives a Porsche."

"I think that's it, then. Is there anything I can do for you?" I asked.

"Keep coming to see me. Please keep coming to see me."

Natalie looked so miserable that there was no way I could have turned her down.

"I'll be back as soon as I have something to report," I promised.

I spent a few more minutes listening to her concerns about Jimmy and Sarah and then said good-bye, pointing out that I had to get to the clinic.

More than that, I had used up my tolerance for being inside the jail. I had never thought of myself as claustrophobic, but there was something about that building that weighed me down. Just being inside as a visitor gave me visions of being entombed alive.

I wanted to run down the path to the gate, but I forced myself to walk. The deputy nodded and smiled as he gave me back my identification. I held my breath until I stepped outside the guardhouse.

The return to the warm January sunshine was a return to life and breath and an open heart. I drove back down the hill to the freeway counting my blessings.

The problems faced by my afternoon clients at the clinic didn't loom quite as large as they might have before Natalie. Both Luisa and Joanna were coping with their lives. I did what I could, then left the clinic.

In the now-fading afternoon sun, I thought about what to do next. I really wanted to go home, but the traffic was already bad, so I figured I could do one more thing first—I could swing by Craig Thorson's old apartment, just to see if it gave me any bright ideas.

The address was on the Westside, on a street that ran a couple of blocks south of Wilshire. I worked my way in that direction, first on Beverly, then Third, then Wilshire.

When I found the building I was looking for, I stopped so suddenly that it took a squeal of brakes and honking horn behind me to break the spell, the contrast with Natalie's neighborhood and house was so great.

Craig's apartment was in a fourplex, bright white stucco with rococo trim, well-tended yard with a barely noticeable sign saying that it was protected by a private security firm. No wonder Natalie was depressed. And no wonder the police thought she had motive for murder.

I parked the car and got out, just to get a closer look. No one was around, and I couldn't think of a good reason to knock on doors.

The area was so attractive that I thought fleetingly of calling the landlord and asking how much the rent would be. But it was also the kind of area where, as they say, if you have to ask...

I got back in my car, swung back to Wilshire, and decided to take Beverly Glen over the hill. The bumper-to-bumper traffic was a little easier to take amid the greenery.

And I thought back to my meeting with Natalie.

Craig Thorson's disabled sister didn't seem too

much of a lawsuit threat. I still wanted to help Natalie, but maybe the threat of a civil suit, the threat to my career, wasn't what I had feared. I just might have overreacted.

My relaxed state lasted only until I reached my own apartment and checked my answering machine. In the middle of four messages from clients was one from someone with a hoarse whisper of undetermined sex.

"Natalie Thorson murdered Craig," the voice said. "There's nothing you can do. Take this as a word to the wise. It's time to stop asking questions."

Or maybe the threat was worse than I feared.

SEVEN

THE THREAT murdered sleep. I couldn't even call Michael to tell him about it, to siphon off some of the anxiety, because Michael had wanted me to stop asking questions before the threat. And I certainly couldn't call Richard, who didn't even know I was asking questions about a murder to begin with.

So I was stuck with myself and an answering machine tape. I listened to it again, hoping that something about the voice would strike me as familiar, but nothing did. I pulled it out and replaced it with a clean tape, with a vague sense that at some point I could turn the message over to the police as evidence.

But I wasn't ready to stop asking questions. Besides, how would this person know whether I had stopped asking questions or not? How did this person even know I was asking questions? Other than Jimmy and Alicia, who seemed to want my help, the only people I had talked with were the ones at the bar.

I didn't think it could be Debbie or the bartender, so the threat had to have come from one of the men at the table. None of them had seemed particularly violent, and none had seemed to be the type to be spending his time keeping an eye on me to see whether I kept asking questions about Craig Thorson.

So if I didn't go back to the bar, and if I could somehow convince Gary Parkman that I wasn't really doing anything big on the case, I ought to be all right. Maybe I could even mention the threat to him, see what he thought.

The rational approach worked for me intellectually, but I still didn't sleep. This wasn't what I had in mind when I hoped for a little excitement.

I was so restless that Amy gave up on me a little after midnight. She withered me with one of her you-know-I-love-you-but-I-need-my-sleep looks and moved to a chair, with Mac dutifully following. I thought about trying to convince him to stay on the bed, but it would only have confused him.

The morning brought light but no clarity.

Julie Thorson was indeed listed in the telephone directory, a Chatsworth address. If she was willing to see me before lunch, I could run over there and back with plenty of time before my first client in the afternoon.

I waited until after nine before I called.

"Helloooo?" A groggy voice drew the word out to three syllables.

"My name is Faith Cassidy," I told her, "and I want to tell you how sorry I am about your brother's murder."

"Who are you?"

"Faith Cassidy. I'm a therapist."

"God, I could use a therapist about now."

"Yes, I'm sure this is a very difficult time for you. I don't know that I can be of any help, but I was wondering if I could come over and talk with you for a few minutes about Craig,'' I said.

"Did you know Craig?" she asked.

"No. I know Natalie, Craig's ex-wife, and I don't believe she murdered him."

"Natalie's a wimp. Natalie couldn't kill anybody."

"Yes, exactly," I said. "And I'm trying to help her prove that. Could I stop by to see you late this morning?"

"Yeah, I guess. Do you know where I live?"

She gave me directions, and I told her I'd be over in an hour.

When you're used to getting in your car and driving in the same direction every time, the direction that takes you over the hills to L.A., you don't always notice how big the Valley is, how far it stretches in three other directions. Huge. The Valley is huge. And it don't get no respect in L.A. No wonder Valleyites wanted to secede and form their own city. Chatsworth is at the far northwest corner of the Valley, some twenty miles of flat freeway driving from where I lived. I made it in less time than I expected, because there wasn't much traffic.

The condo complex was a group of two-story buildings with that faux adobe plus red-tiled roof design that is supposed to look natural, supposed to echo an earlier era, but never does because something about the buildings made them stiff and uncompromising when they should be fluid. The complex was easy to spot from the freeway, but negotiating my way to one of the few guest parking spaces and finding Julie Thorson's unit took some concentration. The buildings all looked alike, and the numbers were so discreetly tacked to the sides of the building that it took me awhile to discover them.

I knocked on her door and waited for a response. I was about to knock again when the door was slowly opened by a woman in a pink silk bathrobe in need of laundering. She held the door with her right hand but leaned heavily on the cane in her left.

"You're the therapist? Come on in."

Julie Thorson was maybe in her early forties, but illness had lined her face. Her short dark hair hadn't been brushed in a while, and her eyes had the glazed look of the long-term tranquilizer user. I looked for a resemblance to Craig Thorson's picture, and found it in her half-smile.

"I'm Faith Cassidy, yes," I said, following her into a dark living room that stank of stale cigarette smoke.

An oversized television set surrounded by shelves stacked with videotapes took up one entire wall. One of the morning talk shows was on, the sound muted. A sofa and two chairs with matching floral prints faced the set. In a jarring redirection of the space, one of the chairs blocked a fireplace. The cool flickering glow of the television images had taken center stage, eclipsing the warmth of the hearth.

The drapes were closed on the corner windows and also on what I guessed would be a sliding door leading to a patio, since all the units had patios. Inside this room day and night would be the same.

"Sit down," Julie said. "Would you like a soda or something?"

A can of something with a lot of caffeine and sugar

sat on a coaster on the coffee table, next to an over-flowing ash tray.

"No, thank you." I sat down in one of the chairs.

Julie took her place on the sofa. She glanced at the muted television regretfully, then turned back to me.

"So what is it you want to talk with me about?" she asked. "Something about Craig?"

"This has to be a difficult time for you," I said, realizing after I started that I had said the same thing on the phone, "and I'm sorry to intrude, I really am, but I'm trying to help Natalie Thorson. I don't believe she murdered your brother."

"But who would murder Craig?" She lit a cigarette, holding the lighter carefully with trembling fingers.

I hoped she would have the courtesy to blow the smoke in the other direction. She didn't. She exhaled right at me as she continued.

"I don't know what I'm going to do now, I really don't," she said.

"I'm sure it's a terrible loss," I said, smiling as I took a shallow breath.

"Oh, honey, you don't know. Ever since I fell and hurt my back, Craig's been paying the rent for me. I told him I'd pay him back once the legal stuff is worked out, but my attorney doesn't want to settle until we know how bad it is, what my total medical bills are going to look like, how long I'm going to be disabled." If her eyes were an indication, she was going to be disabled for a long time.

And she had an attorney. What's one lawsuit more or less when you already have an attorney?

"When was the last time you saw Craig?" I asked.

"The Sunday before he was killed. He stopped by to see me every Sunday, see if I needed anything, leave me some money," she said. "We were always close, even when we were kids. He was five years older than me, and he always took care of me. The situation with our parents wasn't so good, but we had each other."

"Did he talk to you about what was going on in his life?"

"Always. Always told me how well he was doing, too, which is what I don't understand. I'm the heir, Craig left everything to me, and my attorney is having trouble finding Craig's assets, he says. How could he have trouble finding assets?" She looked at me as if she really expected an answer.

"Is it possible that Craig painted a rosier picture of his financial situation than was actually the case?" I asked.

"What? You think he lied to me? No. Craig wouldn't lie to me. To somebody else, maybe, but not to me. The assets are there." She was adamant. And she punctuated the last sentence with puffs of smoke.

"Natalie seems to think he was broke," I said.

"Yeah, well, Craig maybe had reason to lie to Natalie, didn't think he ought to pay what Natalie wanted in the divorce, and all that," Julie said. "So maybe he hid his assets or something, got them tied up so Natalie couldn't find them. But the money is somewhere, I keep telling my attorney, the money is somewhere."

I thought back to that Westside apartment. I suspected Julie was right.

"Well, if Craig wasn't worried about money, did he seem worried about anything else the last time you saw him?" I asked.

"No. In fact, I had the idea that he met somebody new, that he was excited about somebody." She exhaled heavily, and her eyes filled with tears. "Oh, God, honey. Craig was such a wonderful guy. How am I going to survive?"

I reached over and took her hand.

"Is there anyone besides Craig who could help you out for a while?" I asked.

"Nobody. I used to have friends, but after I got hurt, everybody stopped coming to see me. I don't know what happened." The tears flooded down her cheeks.

"Julie, you have to hang on," I said firmly. "You have a doctor, you have an attorney, and you have to ask them to help you rebuild your support system. Under the circumstances, your attorney would probably be able to make a case that a therapist's bills should be included in your medical expenses in the lawsuit."

"I'm seeing a therapist. He says I have reason to be depressed, just keep taking my pills."

"What are you taking?"

"I got a bunch. Every doctor gives you something different, you know." Her eyes wandered to the television set, then back to me.

"Julie, mixing prescriptions isn't a good idea."

"But it helps the time go by, the time go by until I'm well," she whispered.

If she were my client, I might have tried to argue with her, argue that numbing herself wasn't the way to get well, that the way to get well was to fight for her health. But she wasn't my client, and for all I knew she was better served by her therapist than she was telling me. This could be a bid for my sympathy, after all. And I had a gut feeling that giving it to her wouldn't help either of us.

So I went back to my reason for being there.

"Did Craig mention the name of the new woman in his life?" I asked.

"No. He didn't even really say there was some-body, he just hinted," she said, wiping tears away.

"I don't suppose you have any idea who might have wanted to murder him," I said.

That started the tears again. I squeezed her hand, feeling guilty.

"None. Absolutely none."

I stayed for a few more minutes, hoping to bring a small amount of cheer to the conversation, but there didn't seem to be a bright spot in Julie Thorson's life. I said good-bye when I realized that I was going to have to rush to make it home in time to eat something before my first client of the afternoon was due.

When I got outside, I took my first deep breath since Julie lit her cigarette. I could feel little bits of smoke and tar clinging to the inside of my sinuses. And I would have to change my clothes when I got home.

I thought about the conversation as I negotiated the

freeways. Surely Craig Thorson couldn't have been seriously involved with the hooker. So there had to be someone else, and he didn't seem the type to hide his amorous affairs. Someone would know who she was.

And then there was the question of the money. If he had indeed hidden assets, that gave Natalie even more reason to murder him. But it also had to provide motive for any of the clients whose portfolios were destroyed, especially women who felt doubly betrayed. I had to be able, somehow, to find out who they were.

I could follow the money to murder. I felt a momentary shiver at the idea. Follow the money to murder. Almost a game, not follow the leader, but follow the murder.

On the other hand, though, if there were hidden assets, they might be a reason for the threatening message I received. The person who left it might have nothing to do with the murder. He—and I had decided it was a he—might simply know something about the assets and want them for himself. Thus, he wouldn't want anyone asking questions about Craig Thorson.

A rational thought that left me emotionally unsatisfied and nervous. I shoved aside the problem of the threat.

Besides, my best bet for more information on all fronts was that evening's dinner with Gary Parkman.

The afternoon was a long one. Of my three clients, one was a college student seeing me for the first time who didn't know what she wanted to do with her life, one was a married woman having an affair while her marriage fell apart who didn't know what she wanted to do with her life, and one was an attorney in the throes of a midlife crisis, including a dissolving marriage, who didn't know what she wanted to do with her life.

After my last client left, I fed Amy and Mac and then looked through my closet to find something to wear to dinner. Gary Parkman would be coming from work, so he would be dressed like a grown-up. That didn't mean I had to dress in kind, of course, but dressing either too casual or too flirty would call too much attention to my clothes.

I settled on dark green pants and a matching jacket with a nice kind of loose flow and a white silk blouse, with chunky gold jewelry. The pants suit was left over from the days when I occasionally had to take a meeting, and I rarely wore it, but the classic lines would work for this evening.

I left the apartment with what I thought was plenty of time to make it to the restaurant, since I would be going against the traffic. There is, however, no such thing as "against the traffic" on Friday, and when I pulled up to the Valet Parking sign, I was fifteen minutes late.

I turned my car over to a kid in a red vest who had the good sense to smile at me. Somebody dumb would have sneered at the car, which was surely the oldest and least expensive he would see that evening.

The restaurant was a large one, but it created the illusion of cozy by breaking up the area with columns and levels. Although it was early for dinner by L.A. standards, most of the tables were already taken. Corporate and financial types, from the conservative style of dress. No Industry artists in this bunch.

The maitre d' stood professionally poised until I walked over and told him what I was doing there, and then informed me that Mr. Parkman was waiting in the bar.

By the look of his rosy face and red-rimmed blue eyes, Mr. Parkman had been waiting for at least two martinis.

"Hey, Fay," he said, flashing a dimpled smile, "you look great. What'll you have?"

"Chardonnay is fine," I said.

He waved at the bartender and ordered a bottle of a Napa Valley Chardonnay that I knew only by reputation.

"We'll have the rest of it at dinner," he said, when I started to object.

The bartender went through the ritual of letting me taste it before he poured a full glass. I was glad Gary had stopped my objection. The Chardonnay was rich, oaky, fruity, everything I ever dreamed of in a wine, the kind of wine you know you ought to sip, but so good that you want to keep tasting it, one sip after another. It was so good that for a moment I was glad I had met Gary Parkman.

I smiled at him, and I meant it.

"Yeah," he said, smiling back. "It's a nice little wine. I like it that you appreciate wine."

"I do appreciate wine. And I'm sorry I was late."

"Coming from the Valley? Somebody coming from four blocks would be late on a Friday night. You did fine."

"Thank you." I tried to think of a way to make small talk until we got to the table, but the only thing I wanted to talk about was the reason I was there. "We didn't get much chance to talk the other night. How well did you know Craig Thorson?"

Gary Parkman's smile became a little less cheerful, a little rigid even, his eyes cooler.

"Your business card says you're a therapist," he said. "Why are you pretending to be a detective?"

"I'm not a detective. And I'm not pretending I am," I said. "You somehow jumped to that conclusion at the bar."

"Because you were asking questions about a murder. Why do you want to know about Craig Thorson?"

"I know Natalie Thorson, I don't believe she killed her ex-husband, and nobody else seems to be asking questions."

"Okay." Gary nodded, still with the smile that didn't reach his eyes. "Tell you what. Let's have a pleasant dinner, and I'll talk about Craig over coffee."

"Fair enough." So I had to ask about him. We had to talk about something. "Tell me about your business, then. Your card says you're vice-president of a bank, Investors Mutual I think it said, but you hang out with stockbrokers. Do you do a lot of business with them?"

"A lot," he answered, good humor returning. "I was a stockbroker until the 1987 crash, but then I decided I wanted something with a steadier paycheck. I regretted leaving for a while during the nineties, but

I think I made the right decision. Investors Mutual is a small, private bank, which makes me a big fish in it. I deal mostly with corporate accounts, not individuals, and I don't try to sell them anything. Fewer ulcers that way."

I tried to think of a follow-up question, but the best I could come up with was, "With the ups and downs of the financial markets, I'd think ulcers came with the territory, even working for a bank, unless you have a stomach of steel."

"Well, it's not steel, but I have a private theory that alcohol neutralizes stomach acid." He took another sip of his martini to emphasize the point.

I smiled.

"So how did you get from being an actress to being a therapist?" he asked.

"When I lost the *Coffee Time* gig, my television career was over. Nobody wanted to hire me. I got from being an actress to being a therapist by going to graduate school."

"Yeah? Do you miss TV?"

"I did. I don't anymore," I replied. "I like what I do now."

"Does that include your social life?"

I tried frantically to think of a way to turn the conversation to some kind of neutral ground. I couldn't ask enough questions about him, because I wasn't that interested in him, and I didn't want to talk about me for the next hour. Not that I mind talking about myself with friends. But this man wasn't a friend, and something about him—the disconnect between his eyes and his mouth added to the suspicion that he might be an alcoholic—led to an intuitive feeling that he never would be a friend.

"My social life is fairly quiet," I said. "And what do you like to do when you're not working?"

"Eat and drink," he said. "I eat and drink. And sometimes I spend a weekend in Las Vegas, just to remind myself of the difference between the stock market and real gambling."

It was going to be a long dinner.

I have to say, though, that the meal was the best I had eaten in a while, linguini in a light tomato sauce with prawns, clams, and mussels, the kind of Italian food that reminds one of why everyone loves Italian food. I concentrated on my own dinner so that I could ignore Gary's, which was a thick veal chop.

I had to work to ignore it because I didn't want to bring up the subject of where veal comes from and how the calves are treated, since I needed Gary in a friendly enough mood to answer my questions. And the wine helped. I carefully nursed my second glass so I wouldn't drink too much of the wine.

But the conversation never really got going. The best I could do was get him talking about his ex-wives, and why he never wanted to get married again, which had everything to do with money, and nothing to do with love.

Finally, with cappuccinos and small cups of chocolate mousse in front of each of us, and a brandy snifter in his hand, Gary said, "Okay. What do you want to know about Craig Thorson?"

"Anything you can tell me that might explain why someone other than his ex-wife would murder him,"

I replied. "I'm particularly interested in knowing what women might be angry with him, or what business associates might feel unfairly treated. Especially if there's an overlap."

He chuckled. "You know the difference between a rooster and a stockbroker? A rooster clucks defiance."

"How many clients would we be talking about in Craig Thorson's case?" I asked, forcing a smile at the lame joke.

"Recently? Or in his entire career?" Gary asked.

"Let's say within the last year."

He thought for a moment.

"I'd say two, maybe three, but you have to remember, I didn't work with Thorson, I only knew him socially, by what he said at the bar. He dropped a lot of hints, nothing more. So if you're looking for names, I can't help you," he said.

"What about the hooker he brought to the bar—Tory somebody?" I asked, keeping the annoyance out of my voice.

"What about her?" Gary chuckled again. He had kind of a cute chuckle for such an annoying man. Even if it didn't reach his eyes.

"I heard he brought her in on some kind of bet."

"Debbie told you that? Not a bet, exactly, but a kind of joke. Tory got paid, and she seemed to have a good time. She didn't kill Craig Thorson, or anybody else."

"You say you didn't work with Craig Thorson. Does that mean none of his clients had accounts with you?" I asked.

The eyes got colder. "I couldn't answer that one if I wanted to. Fiduciary responsibility to keep things confidential."

"Okay." It wasn't, but I let it go. "Do you have any idea how Thorson was doing financially—just from your social interaction with him?"

"Hard to tell. The rumor was that he was highly leveraged, which is a nice way of saying broke. But he spent it like he had it," Gary replied, still with the cold eyes.

"If somebody like Thorson wanted to hide assets, how would he do it?"

Gary shrugged. He was getting restless, and his tone became cooler with every answer. "Probably offshore, like everybody else."

"Someone saw Craig Thorson arguing with a man in a Porsche. Do you have any idea who the man could have been?" I didn't want to bring Natalie's son into the conversation.

"Somebody in a Lexus or a Mercedes, maybe. Not a Porsche." The tight smile let me know it was Gary's idea of humor.

"Okay. Just one more question. Can you think of any reason why one of the guys at the table the other night would be so upset because I was asking questions that he would threaten me?"

"Somebody threatened you?"

The surprise was genuine. I believed it.

"Sort of. Somebody left a message on my answering machine telling me to stop asking questions." Telling him made me uncomfortable. I almost wished I hadn't brought the threat up.

"If one of those guys called you, it was a joke," he said firmly.

I would have to listen to the message again. It hadn't sounded like a joke.

Gary caught the waiter's eye and signaled for the check.

"Sorry I haven't been of much help," he said. "I didn't know Thorson's ex-wife, but I have to say that she's as likely to have offed him as anybody else. And since the police had enough evidence to arrest her, maybe whoever called you is right. Maybe you ought to stop asking questions."

Maybe I ought to, but I wasn't ready to.

Although I wasn't certain what my next move was, beyond getting rid of Gary Parkman.

That turned out to be easier than I feared. The questions about Craig Thorson had soured his mood. Gary finished his brandy, pocketed his credit card, and walked me out to the valet parking area.

Just as the kid in the red vest brought my car, I realized I did have one more question for Gary Parkman.

"You think it's the money, don't you? You think somebody knifed Craig Thorson over money, not sex," I said. "A crime of passion, but not in the way most of us think about it."

Gary tried for his cute chuckle, but didn't make it.

"I don't know, Fay. But I'm not going to worry about it, and you shouldn't, either." He handed the kid a folded bill and held the car door for me. "Good to see you. And good luck in your new career."

I barely managed to thank him for the meal before he shut the door and walked away.

EIGHT

SATURDAY MORNING brought me no new ideas and certainly no answers. The only person who would tell me whatever she knew about Craig Thorson's business dealings was Natalie, and she obviously didn't know much, especially where the possibility of hidden assets was concerned. Still, at some point I would have to ask her.

But that meant another trip to Sybil Brand, and I wasn't up for another trip, not on Saturday. I had four clients coming, and then I was having dinner with Richard, and I was no closer to straightening out my feelings about Richard—not to mention Cydnee— than I had been on Tuesday.

In fact, as I sat there on my deck, latte in hand, looking out on the wildly gorgeous green leaves of the tree next door, with Amy and Mac curled up on the blue-and-white striped cushion of the redwood chaise, I had two thoughts. The first was that I was quite comfortable without Richard, thank you very much. The second was that I ached without Richard, and some of my running around for Natalie was really to keep from feeling the ache.

I got distracted from the ache when it hit me that Richard and I had both assumed that dinner would be in Silver Lake, not Sherman Oaks, that I would drive to his place, not he to mine. In fact, he had never come to my new apartment.

I picked up the phone.

"Can we meet out here tonight?" I asked when Richard answered.

"Is this some kind of a test?"

"No. I just don't feel like driving that far," I said.

"This feels like some kind of test, but okay, I'll come there. Give me directions."

I gave him directions, and we agreed on seven o'clock. I knew he'd be late. One of the reasons I always drove there was a practical one. Like Thoreau, Richard saw time as but a stream he goes a-fishing in, or in Richard's case, a-painting in. It could flow right by, and he took very little notice of the flow. When I arrived, he could stop working. Tonight he was on his own.

Another practical reason I drove to Silver Lake was that we both knew the restaurants there, the neighborhood places where we could count on relatively inexpensive good food. Still, if I was going to live in the Valley, I was going to have to learn to eat here. And there were some places on Ventura Boulevard that looked worth trying.

I pulled out the telephone directory and started flipping through the restaurant listings. In Silver Lake we might be able to eat without reservations. Not in Sherman Oaks. In fact, I had to try four of the interesting-looking places before I found one that would take us, and that wasn't until nine. I considered calling Richard back to tell him he could safely be late. I didn't.

The thought of dinner made me hungry. I toasted a couple of frozen blueberry waffles and sliced some fresh strawberries to eat with them. Even in January, fresh strawberries came in from the Central California fields. One of the small pleasures that made mornings worth looking forward to.

Food taken care of, I got ready for my first appointment.

All things considered, it was an easy day. Three of my clients were lonely women who just needed someone to talk to. In another day, or another city, they would have had friends to confide in, or relatives to live with, but they had somehow gotten lost in L.A. The only thing I could do for them, besides listening to the week's report, was advise them to go out and meet people, try to form a support system. The fourth had serious health problems and really did need a neutral sounding board as she sorted out her options for treatment.

But nobody was being sued, and nobody was being threatened, and at the end of the afternoon I was still feeling pretty good.

I approached my answering machine, and its blinking light, with only a bit of wariness, conscious of the fact that Gary might have let the wrong person know I was still asking questions.

Two messages from clients, neither urgent, and one from Debbie. No threats.

"I have two names for you," Debbie's voice said. "Roberta Hill—that's right, the actress—and Jane Browning. According to last night's table talk, those are the two prizes worth fighting over from Craig's client list. And I have an appointment to see David Jacobson on Monday. I'll let you know how it goes.''

Roberta Hill, the actress. Aging actress was more like it. I had interviewed her once on *Coffee Time*, when both of us had careers to brag about, although she was fifteen years older than I and far more successful. She had managed to work well into her forties, but her career had taken a nose dive about the time she hit fifty. There had to be a way I could get in touch with her now.

Jane Browning's name was one of those that appeared every now and then in the *Times'* Social Circuits column, when she organized some big charitable fund-raiser. She would be easy to find if I had money to give, but even without making a fat pledge I should be able to find a way to get in touch.

I decided to do quick Internet searches on both to see if an avenue immediately sprang to mind.

As it turned out, finding Roberta Hill was even easier than I expected. She was starring in a revival of *Light Up the Sky* at a small theater in North Hollywood. I could go to the Sunday matinee and wait to see her after the show.

My search on Jane Browning turned up not only the expected references to charitable fund-raisers, but also some news items on a domestic violence complaint and a very messy divorce. The interesting thing about the domestic violence was that Jane had attacked her husband—not with a knife, unfortunately for my purposes. She threw a lamp at him. The cut on his forehead had required ten stitches.

Nothing gave me a clue to where she lived.

But I did find one hint as to where she might be found. The search engine led me to a publication called *DJ News,* in which a female disc jockey chatting about her favorite day spa, Nirvana, mentioned some of the upscale clients who patronized the place, including Jane Browning. Now all I had to do was figure out when she was due for a facial.

And the first step would be to make an appointment for myself. I had treated myself to regular facials when I did *Coffee Time,* to keep the heavy TV makeup from settling into my pores. Then, of course, they were tax-deductible. But that was years ago, and I had given them up—along with a lot of other things—when I was in graduate school. Now I was really, truly ready for one. A quick phone call and I was booked for Monday morning, although the price of the facial was going to bust my budget for the month. The price quoted was almost twice what I used to pay.

That was the extent of my online discoveries.

I changed clothes, poured myself a glass of wine, and wandered back out to the deck to wait for Richard.

He was almost an hour late.

I was nursing a second glass of wine and a serious annoyance when I heard the Harley.

I met him at the door.

"I'm sorry," he said. "I was working, and I needed to get to a good stopping place."

His eyes lacked their usual glow, and there was a slight sag to his clean-shaven cheeks. I relented a little.

"I knew you'd be late," I said. "And anyway, I couldn't get a dinner reservation until nine, so we have plenty of time. Do you want to see the apartment?"

"Sure."

Amy heard his voice, and she was rubbing against his leg before he had taken more than two steps into the living room. Amy liked Richard, something that puzzled Mac, who felt he was supposed to like Richard, too, but he couldn't bring himself to do it.

So when Richard picked Amy up, saying, "Hey, baby, good to see you," I picked Mac up and gave him a hug.

Richard glanced at my Maxfield Parrish poster and looked quickly away. I knew he thought it was too kitschy for words.

"Nice," Richard finally said, as we stood for a moment on the deck. Not that he could see much of the trees or anything. By then, it was dark, and too chilly to stay out for long. Which was just as well, since there was barely room for both of us. The chaise and the pots took up most of the space.

"You don't really like any of it," I said.

"It's okay, just a little flat and characterless after the place you had in Silver Lake. And you don't have a separate space for an office here. Your living room has client vibes in it. I like the deck."

"Okay. I'll get my jacket, and we can go."

I dropped Mac onto a chair, and Richard dropped Amy beside him. I grabbed a jacket and my bag and keys and met Richard at the apartment door.

We both knew we would take my car. Richard followed me down to the garage in silence.

"Where are we eating?" he asked once I had pulled out of the driveway and made a couple of turns, landing us on Ventura Boulevard.

"I made a reservation at a place that looked interesting," I said. "It's Greek. I've never been there."

"Yeah, Greek food sounds good." He said it as if he didn't care.

"Are you okay?" I asked.

"I'm tired, Faith. That's all." He paused, then added, "I've got a gallery showing coming up, and I need to finish what I'm working on this next week."

"That's great," I said. "And the gallery is…?"

I wasn't surprised when he named the one we had been to the week before, the one showing Cydnee's work.

"Do you want to talk about Cydnee's connection with this?" I asked.

"Not really. She brought up the idea with Annie Roper, the gallery owner, but I could have done that myself. I just hadn't gotten around to doing it," he replied.

"No, of course you hadn't." That was a cheap shot, and I immediately regretted it. But Richard was more interested in producing work than selling it, and every time I had tried to encourage him to promote himself more, we had gotten into an argument. "I'm sure Michael would be happy to lend the painting of Elizabeth, if you'd like."

I said it hoping to ease the tension, but Richard flared.

"So I can get commissions doing cat portraits?"

"I was thinking more about demonstrating your range." I didn't bother asking what was wrong with commissions for cat portraits.

"Sorry."

We were about two blocks from the restaurant, and I spotted a parking place. Normally I would have looked for something closer, but parking the car distracted both of us from the conversation.

There was already a chill in the night air. I knew the walk back to the car wouldn't be comfortable, no matter what the next turn in the conversation was.

The restaurant was brightly lit and full of cheerful, noisy people, and I immediately regretted my choice.

Besides, we were early, and that meant waiting at the bar, which didn't help Richard's mood.

I have to give him credit for making an effort, though.

"You know what's happening in my life," he said. "But I haven't heard about yours. How did your week go?"

I ordered a glass of Pinot Grigio, a drinkable wine that would be okay with Greek food, watched the bartender pour it, and took a sip before I answered.

"It's been a little rough," I said, deciding to tell him the truth. "One of my clients has been arrested for murder, and I don't think she did it."

"Don't get involved, Faith."

He sounded so annoyed that it was my turn to flare.

"I am involved, Richard. I couldn't just sit still while my client goes to trial for something she didn't do. That's not who I am."

"No. You're somebody who needs the excitement and the attention of center stage," he said.

"You're right. That's also true. But it doesn't mean that my need to help my client is any less valid. And if you see my need for attention as something so terrible, what are you doing with me?" I could have said something about his need for attention, but it wouldn't have helped.

"It's not terrible, I didn't mean it that way. I'm tired, I told you that, and this probably isn't the best time for a heavy conversation. But as far as what I'm doing with you is concerned..." He let the sentence trail off, which wasn't encouraging. "Love isn't always rational, and we don't always love every trait in somebody's personality. I can be annoyed at something you do and still love you. You can be annoyed at something I do. Does that mean you don't love me?"

"If I didn't love you, I wouldn't be here tonight," I said, and that was as close to absolute truth as anything I know.

"Okay. Then why don't we back off and talk about something else for a while?"

I couldn't ask about books, because Richard doesn't read much. He wasn't likely to have gone to a movie, and he watches television with remote control in hand, so he rarely knows what he's watching. I was left with only one place to go.

"Eaten any good meals lately?" I asked.

He had the grace to laugh.

And I was saved from having to follow that question up by a perky woman with menus who led us to our table, one in the middle of the room, which was so jammed with other small tables that there was barely space enough for a chair on either side.

Richard glanced at me to see how I was going to react.

I shrugged at him and smiled at the perky woman.

The menu was large, the prices fairly reasonable. I decided to try one of those combination plates—hummus, tabouli, falafel, spanakopita, and other stuff—and he went for some kind of chicken.

The food arrived quickly, and I had another glass of wine. Normally I would have enjoyed the variety of tastes and textures that made up my combination plate, but the tension got in the way. Richard's chicken was actually more interesting—the sauce had kalamata olives in it. If I ever came back to the restaurant, and if I hadn't totally given up eating animal flesh by then, I might order it.

We made it through dinner by playing a game, making up stories about the people at the other tables. It was the only thing that could keep us away from our own story.

But dinner came to an end, as everything in life must, and we were left with what to do next.

"How about letting me drive you home?" Richard asked, once we were on the street.

"I can drive just fine," I answered.

"On how many glasses of wine?"

"I've had four, but it's been over an entire evening. I've driven on a lot more than that, and the apartment is only a few blocks." I was ready to get belligerent, and I knew that was a bad sign.

"You've had four, and that's okay, because there are about five glasses in a bottle, and as long as you've had less than a bottle, you're not drinking too much. Right?" He was ready to get belligerent, too.

So I didn't push it. And I drove even more carefully than usual, just to prove that I could do it.

I eased the car carefully into its parking space, turned to him, and smiled triumphantly.

And that brought us to the moment of truth.

"Do you want me to come in?" he asked.

"Not really." I lost the smile.

"Does that mean good-bye?"

"Oh, God, Richard, I still don't know." I leaned my forehead against the steering wheel. "We've somehow gotten into the habit of not resolving problems, of deciding that whatever-it-is isn't important enough to interfere with sex, and now that we're faced with something that is important, I don't know what to do with it."

"You're the therapist. If you don't know, how do you expect me to?"

"I don't expect you to." I lifted my head and looked at him. His face was in shadow, his arms crossed tightly. "All right. This is the best I can do. You're stressed, I'm stressed, and you have a gallery showing coming up. I wouldn't miss your opening for the world. Shall we give it a rest until then?"

He leaned over and kissed me on the cheek.

"I'll call you," he said.

Then he got out of the car and walked away, leaving me sitting there.

And I was still sitting there when I heard the Harley, loud at first, then fading to nothing.

NINE

I DIDN'T SLEEP MUCH. In the morning, I had a dull ache in my heart and a lump in my throat. I hurt too much to call Michael and tell him what had happened. Comfort would have to wait until I was ready to accept it.

Besides, if I called Michael, he would either try to talk me out of going to the matinee to see Roberta Hill, or he would want to go with me, and I didn't want company.

So I dawdled away the hours with the Sunday *Times* and a couple of lattes until it was time to get ready to go.

The theater was on Lankershim, one of a number of small theaters that had sprung up in NoHo, the North Hollywood arts district, in the last few years. There was a used book store on one side and a coffee house on the other, an old-fashioned coffee house that advertised open mike poetry readings on Monday nights.

The area reminded me a little of Silver Lake, except with straight streets and no hills. And the apartment buildings were all made of concrete and stucco, with flat surfaces. No quaint bungalows with yards in that part of the Valley.

There was, of course, a parking problem. The parking god must have taken Sunday off, because I had to park three blocks away and walk.

I hadn't been expecting much, which was a good thing. I had been expecting a real theater, though, and what I found was a converted retail space, with only curtains to separate the lobby from the stage. A friendly young man behind a counter with a cash register that appeared to be left over from the building's previous incarnation took my money and told me to go on in and take any seat.

I picked up a program, actually a single folded piece of paper, and slipped between the dark curtains.

Enough folding chairs to seat sixty or seventy people were set up on three sides of a square that held a rudimentary set—a back flat with a mirror and table next to a door, a small sofa and a couple of chairs around a coffee table, and a bird cage with a stuffed parrot.

The young man meant it when he told me to take any seat. Curtain time was in fifteen minutes, and there were only four other people in the room. They were sitting front row center, marking them as friends of somebody in the cast.

I sat down in the fourth row, off to one side, hoping that more people would arrive at the last minute. I never had to give a performance when the cast outnumbered the audience, but I knew it had to be demoralizing. I wondered what on earth Roberta Hill was doing in this place.

The program didn't answer that question, but it did hold an annoying surprise. When my Internet search turned up the play, I hadn't checked the other members of the cast. One of them, Van Lawrence, was a man I'd had a weekend fling with, during what Sam Melman had referred to as my weird period.

I'm always amazed at just how small the theatrical community in Southern California is. Of course, I've lived here all of my life, I graduated from a major university with a degree in theater, I'd interviewed a wide range of people, including actors plugging shows, during five years on *Coffee Time*, I'd eaten at restaurants both trendy and funky more times than I cared to imagine, I'd gone to more parties than I cared to remember, and I had to have met, interviewed, slept with, or somehow crossed paths with a ton of actors. Thus, I shouldn't be surprised when I run into somebody I know in a North Hollywood theater.

Nevertheless, I was unsettled at the thought of seeing Van Lawrence. I wondered if there was a way I could see Roberta Hill after the play without having to see him as well. In a theater this small, I doubted it. I had a fleeting hope he wouldn't remember me, but he surely would.

We had met at a mutual friend's birthday party, where there was a variety of drinks and drugs to suit everyone's taste. He had been hitting on me for much of the evening, and I finally said, "Look, Van, forget it. I don't want to have another one-night stand."

Van, startled, replied, "Most women would have said, 'I don't want to *be* another one-night stand.' I'll tell you what—let's make it a *two*-night stand. I'm free for the weekend."

I was so zonked out of my head that I thought he

was funny, and I said yes. We spent the weekend so stoned that I barely made it to the television station Monday morning. Although I have to emphasize that I did make it, on time and ready to work. That was seven years ago, and I hadn't seen Van again from that day to this.

I already felt sorry for Roberta Hill, reduced to this makeshift theater from what had once been a solid career. The knowledge that she was working with Van Lawrence tripled my compassion for her.

My spirits improved slightly about five minutes before curtain time, when a handful of people trickled in. At fifteen minutes after the scheduled time, when the lights finally went down, there were maybe twenty people in the audience.

Light Up the Sky is one of those old war horses by Kaufman and Hart that community theaters love to put back in harness partly because audiences still laugh at the jokes but at least as much because it gives middle-aged actors juicy roles. By the time Roberta Hill made her entrance, I understood why she was willing to work in this tiny, storefront theater.

Her part was that of an over-the-hill prima donna who had taken a chance on an unglamorous role in an experimental play. And Roberta Hill was clearly having a marvelous time in the role.

She had never been a classic beauty, but she was tall and slender, and she had the kind of presence on stage that made you believe she was a star. Her hair was now a dark honey blond, a shade that still-youthful women use to cover gray, but rarely attractively. In Roberta Hill's case, though, it worked. And her large brown eyes, with the exaggerated eyelashes, were perfect for the broad, period comedy.

I was astounded at the overall quality of the cast, including Van Lawrence, who played the producer. I had seen him in some small television roles, and I had to admit that he was better on stage, willing to emphasize a slight paunch and a receding hairline because they worked for the character, as did his fleshy jowls. I felt better about having slept with him now that I knew he was talented.

The play ended happily, of course, with great reviews for the young playwright's experimental play and the Roberta Hill character's comeback.

All twenty of us rose to our feet in applause for the cast.

I thought about asking the young man who had taken my money how to get backstage, but I decided that following the four people in the front row would get me there sooner. When they walked across the set and through the door in the flat, I followed.

The backstage area consisted of about two feet of space between the stage and the wall. There were stairs at one end, however, and the five of us climbed to the second floor, which had been curtained into a lounge area and two dressing rooms.

I stood off to one side while one of the women poked her head between curtains to let the actress playing the producer's ice-skater wife know they were there. With luck, Roberta Hill would emerge before Van Lawrence did.

I wasn't lucky.

I tried to duck when Van swept out of the curtains

that defined the men's dressing room and headed toward the stairs, but he automatically greeted me with a fast, "Hi, honey," and then stopped short, with a double take straight out of vaudeville.

"Fay Cassidy," he said, pulling me into a bear hug. He partially released me, keeping his hands on my shoulders. "A little heavier, not quite as blond as you used to be, but it suits you. You look healthy. How are you?"

"I'm, uh, fine, Van. I enjoyed the show. How are you?" His greeting was so far from anything I imagined that I wasn't sure how to react. I didn't tell him I'd changed my name because I hoped I wouldn't be around him long enough for it to make any difference.

"Living the good Valley life," he said, his smile showing off teeth so white they had to be caps. "Married, selling cars, doing an occasional play. I lost track of you when I didn't see you on television anymore. What are you doing? What brings you here?"

I was beginning to wonder just how stoned I had been that weekend. Had we parted as bosom buddies? Had we sworn eternal friendship?

"I live in the Valley, too," I said, glad in that moment that I did, because it gave me a reasonable excuse for being there. "I was looking for something pleasant to do this afternoon, and I noticed Roberta Hill was in the play—and you, of course—so I thought I'd stop by."

"You know Bobbie? Listen, some of us are going across the street to the Italian deli, grab a sandwich, you have to join us. Let me tell her you're here." He dropped his hands from my shoulders and took the few steps over to the women's curtain before I could protest.

"Bobbie?" he called. "Fay Cassidy's here, wanted to say hello, so I've invited her to join us. How long are you going to be?"

Roberta Hill stuck her head out, swiveled it until she saw me, then offered a brief nod and a smile. Without the eyelashes, a lot of the star quality was gone.

"Oh, good. I'll be out in just a minute," she said.

"We'll meet you over there," Van said. He came back to me and added, "Come on. I need a cigarette. No smoking in here, no smoking in the deli, I have to get to the street."

I followed Van down the stairs and back through the theater to the tiny lobby, then waited while he said goodnight to the young man.

"If you'd told me you were a friend of Van's, I would have comped you," the young man told me.

"No, no," I assured him. "I was happy to pay. The show was worth it."

Once outside, Van lit his cigarette.

I tried to figure out which way was downwind, guessed wrong, and had to move.

"That's right," Van said, "you never did smoke cigarettes. I don't do any of the other stuff anymore, but this habit I couldn't kick. How about you?"

"Nothing but a little wine. I lead a very different life now."

Three cast members came out of the building and headed toward the corner. One called to Van, "You coming?"

"We'll be along," he said. "We're waiting for Bobbie."

I smiled and nodded. The good thing about running into Van was that this would make it easier for me to work my way into conversation with Roberta Hill. The bad thing—well, Van seemed to have changed, and I had my fingers crossed that he had changed enough so he wouldn't embarrass me by bringing up how we met.

"So what else is going on?" Van asked. "Married?"

"No. I guess I'll always be a free spirit." I had a twinge, thinking of Richard, as I said it.

Roberta—I couldn't think of her as Bobbie—came out of the theater, dressed in jeans and an oversized sweatshirt, large canvas bag slung over her shoulder.

"Come on," she said. "I'm starved."

"I loved the play," I told her. "You were wonderful. Everyone was wonderful."

"It was good of you to come," she said. "We've been having a lot of fun, but the audiences haven't exactly flocked to the show."

"You knew this wasn't the Ahmanson when you signed on, Bobbie," Van said.

She nodded. "No regrets."

The three of us walked to the corner to cross at the light. Lankershim Boulevard is not the kind of street where one can jaywalk.

The deli was half sandwich, salad, and espresso bar, half grocery store. The grocery section appeared to have some interesting imported goodies. I would have to come back another time and check it out. The cast members who had preceded us were seated at one of the few tables, already eating.

Roberta, Van, and I ordered our sandwiches, which came on freshly baked Italian rolls, picked out our salads from the display in the case, and waited for the lone man behind the counter to fix our plates and take our money.

Once we were all seated and eating, the five of them talked mostly about the play, about each other, about people they knew in common, and I decided to put my head down and concentrate on my sandwich—roasted peppers and melted cheese and other good stuff—without drawing attention to myself. The other three drew a blank when Van introduced me, which made it easy.

Concentrating on the sandwich also made it possible for me to almost ignore the unexpected pain I felt sitting there with five people who were in a play, when I hadn't done one in more than ten years. Doing morning television had made the idea of night rehearsals unattractive, and besides, television had in many ways used the same creative energy that would have gone into a play, even though the part I played was more or less myself.

Then when I went to graduate school, I lived in a different world. With all the life changes, I didn't think about doing a play, and I hadn't thought about it since, until I sat there in the deli, licking melted cheese off my fingers, listening to five people who were having a grand time doing a play in a makeshift theater solely for their own benefit and for the entertainment of a handful of people, mostly friends.

I was envious. I hoped it didn't show.

Keeping my head down and eating turned out to be the right choice for another reason. I was finished with my food when Roberta, who had only eaten half of hers, wrapped up the other half of the sandwich in a napkin.

"I have to go," she said. "Have a good week, guys, and I'll see you all on Friday."

"I have to go, too," I said. "I really enjoyed the play. And it was great to see you again, Van."

"Great to see you, Fay. Keep in touch."

I gave what I hoped was a noncommittal smile and caught up with Roberta just as she reached the front door.

"Which way are you going?" I asked.

"My car is parked on the next block over, behind the theater," she said.

"Great. Mine is in that direction. I'll walk with you." As we headed toward the corner, I tried to think of how I could swing the conversation to Craig Thorson.

"How did you come to be in this play?" I asked, just to keep things going.

"I needed some distraction from my life." She gave a little laugh, but the words were serious.

"I understand. I've been there. It was a rough adjustment for me when I left television, and then I lost some money in the stock market." I had to take the shot.

Roberta stopped short.

"All right, Fay," she said, looking me straight in the eye and blasting me with star power. "What do you really want to talk with me about? I do have to be somewhere, so make it fast.''

"Craig Thorson's murder," I said, sighing. "I know his ex-wife, and I don't believe she did it, and so I'm kind of nosing around other people who knew him."

"And how did you get my name in connection with Craig Thorson?''

"I was told that the vultures picking over his accounts referred to yours as one of the prizes.'' I fought the desire to cringe. I had to plant my feet firmly in order not to back away from her in disgrace.

Roberta laughed and shook her head.

"My account is no prize, not anymore. They think I was sleeping with Craig, don't they?"

I could feel my face turning red. I didn't have to answer.

"Well, they're wrong," she continued. "I didn't have an affair with Craig Thorson, although I'm sure he wanted his buddies to think I did. That's the kind of sleazy thing he'd do.''

"If you weren't having an affair with him, why did you let him handle your money?'' I asked.

"Believe it or not, I thought he knew what he was doing. He talked a very good investment line.'' She shifted her canvas bag. "I ended up disliking him intensely. But I didn't kill him, and if his ex-wife didn't kill him, I don't know who did. And now I have to go.''

She walked away swiftly, body language telegraphing that I was not to follow.

By the time I reached my car, I was thoroughly

depressed. I hadn't thought that Roberta Hill would break down sobbing and admit she had stabbed Craig Thorson in a fit of uncontrollable rage, or anything like that, but I had been carried away by my own concerns to the point where I had believed she would at least want to cooperate, care whether the right person went to trial.

Another episode like this one, and I wouldn't need Michael—or a telephoned threat, joke or not—to talk me out of asking more questions.

There was, of course, a message from Michael on my answering machine.

"No phone call this morning, and you're not there this afternoon," his voice said. "I gather things went well last night. Call when you surface for air."

I decided to call him in the morning, after a good night's sleep, when I could put everything in perspective. In the morning, I would have something to look forward to, the facial at Nirvana, and I wouldn't have to ask about Jane Browning if I didn't want to.

But in the morning I had still another unpleasant surprise. According to the *Times*, Gary Parkman had been found dead in his apartment on Sunday, cause unknown.

TEN

THE ARTICLE WAS in the Valley section, below the fold on page eight. I would have missed it if I'd been in a hurry, and I wouldn't have seen it at all if I'd lived in Silver Lake. Gary Parkman, it turned out, lived in Toluca Lake. Another Valley resident, a wealthy one, known for his social connections and charitable activities, according to the report.

If he weren't dead, I would have been annoyed that he asked me to drive all the way to the Westside for dinner when he lived in the Valley.

He was supposed to meet three friends for golf on Sunday morning. I recognized one of the names, Jason Kohl, as the other middle-aged man at the table at Halloran's. When Gary didn't show up at tee time, and no one answered either his apartment phone or his cell phone, they drove to the building, discovered his car in its normal space, and convinced the manager to let them in.

Gary's body was on the bathroom floor, with no obvious signs of foul play. The police had no comment until they could look at an autopsy report, although one of his neighbors said police had asked if anyone had been seen coming or going the night before.

His golf partners, of course, were stunned. As far as they knew, Gary was in perfect health.

Nobody mentioned his heavy drinking.

I picked up the phone and called Michael.

"Gary Parkman's dead," I told him.

"Who's Gary Parkman?"

"I guess I haven't kept you up to date on the Natalie Thorson situation," I said.

"I guess you haven't," he replied.

I filled him in on my trip to the bar, Julie Thorson, my dinner with Gary, Debbie's information, and my brief conversation with Roberta Hill. I left out only the threat on my answering machine.

"And now Gary Parkman's dead. I hope to God he drank too much and hit his head on the wash basin. I can't deal with the possibility that he was murdered," I finished.

"I know that certain of our mutual friends believe that there are no accidents, there are no coincidences, and that everything has a higher meaning, in which case his death, one way or another, is a message for you," Michael said. "But I think some things are random, and sometimes a cigar is just a cigar."

"Freud didn't say that, you know," I stuck in.

"I don't care. What I'm saying is, I don't think you ought to be upset quite yet. Odds are that this really is a coincidence, that the guy had a heart attack or a stroke. Or got drunk and hit his head. Or made the mistake of taking a sleeping pill after drinking a bottle of wine. And that his death has nothing to do with your questions."

"I hope you're right. I'm afraid you're not."

"Do you think you can stay reasonably sane until the results of the autopsy are released?" Michael asked.

"Oh, God, I don't know. I don't feel sane now. And your message about Saturday night was way off, by the way. It was a disaster. I don't think Richard and I are seeing each other anymore." My voice cracked. "I think my whole life is a disaster."

"You think your whole life is a disaster about once a month, Faith, and you know it." When I didn't respond to that, he added, "Do you want to have lunch and talk some more?"

"Can we do it tomorrow? I have that facial scheduled for this afternoon, and I really need to go to Sybil Brand and talk to Natalie about what's happened." The realization that I had something to do was more calming than Michael's verbal slap. Besides, he was wrong. I don't think my life is a disaster more than a couple of times a year.

"Tomorrow would be fine. I approve of the facial, especially if you can refrain from asking questions about the murder, and I suppose you can't leave Natalie in the lurch."

"I don't want to leave Natalie in the lurch," I said firmly. "And anyway, you may be right. Gary Parkman may have had a random heart attack, in which case I can't let his death affect what I'm doing."

"I take it back," Michael said, sighing. "Gary Parkman's death is a sign you should stop asking questions about the murder. Really."

"Sorry. I'll tell you more at lunch tomorrow."

I wasn't thrilled about another trip to Sybil Brand. But at least Natalie would know I was trying to help.

The drive to the jail took more energy than I had to spare, but I discovered that the institution itself wasn't weighing me down quite as much as it had on the first two visits. I had learned to shield myself in some way from the emotional blast of pain and depression that would otherwise be overwhelming. I still didn't understand how the deputies could walk through the gate every day, though. And I did understand why Natalie wanted out so badly.

She looked the same as she had the last time I saw her, neither better nor worse. Not depressed, but not engaged, either. I wished I could get her more involved in her own defense.

"Well, of course Julie would think Craig had hidden assets," Natalie said, once I had explained the purpose of my visit. "Julie has to think that or commit suicide. It's been two years since she fell and hurt her back, and the attorney says she can't settle as long as she has ongoing medical bills. You've seen her, you know what's happened. She goes from doctor to doctor, collecting drug after drug, and she lives her life in a daze. Without Craig, what hope does she have of paying the rent? Or eating?"

Natalie was hardly the one to accuse another of living her life in a daze, but this wasn't the moment to point that out.

"Did you know a man named Gary Parkman?" I asked.

"I don't think so. Why?"

"Because I had dinner with him Friday night, to

talk about Craig, and then he died Saturday night," I said. "It may be a coincidence, having nothing to do with this, of course. There hasn't been an autopsy report, and there was no sign of foul play."

"Oh, Faith, you're not putting yourself in any danger are you?" Her face screwed up, and I was afraid she was going to cry.

"No, Natalie, I'm not. Really."

"Good." Her face relaxed, then twisted again. "Because I couldn't stand it if you had to stop helping me. You're all I have. My mother can't raise bail, and the attorney thinks I may be guilty. My kids don't want to see me. And I'm scared I'll never get out of here."

"I'll do what I can, Natalie. I promise," I said, even though I didn't really like the idea that she saw me as her only hope. The savior complex is a danger for therapists, and I was determined not to fall into that trap. People have to save themselves. But there would be a better time to point that out to Natalie. "Are you sure there isn't some way Craig could have concealed some financial assets?"

"Am I sure? How can I be sure? Of course he could have, anybody who has connections can. But my attorney couldn't find any trace, and if Julie's can't either, then I don't know what to tell you," she said.

I stayed a little longer, because Natalie was so desperate to have me there, but she still didn't remember anyone Craig had fought with, and she didn't have anything helpful to add. I left as soon as I could—

my shield against the institutional pain and depression, and Natalie's naked need, was starting to slip.

I had time to kill before my facial, so I decided to swing by and see how Jimmy and Alicia were doing.

That meant going closer to Richard's apartment than I wanted to be at the moment, but I wanted to check on the two of them enough to do it anyway.

The little house looked shut up tight, but the battered Honda was in the driveway, so I walked up to the door and knocked. I had to knock a second time before Alicia answered.

"Yeah?" she said, making no move to invite me in.

"I just came from a visit with Natalie," I said, "and I wanted to see how Jimmy is doing."

"He's fine. He hasn't remembered anything that would help you. And I can't ask you in just now." She said it so firmly, I knew there was no point in arguing.

"The point is not to help me," I said. "The point is to help his mother."

"He knows that." Alicia stared at me through the screen door as if I were an enemy.

"Tell him I stopped by," I said, backing away.

"I will," she answered, shutting the door before I was off the porch.

When I reached the car, I got in and took a deep breath before I started the engine. I needed that facial, and I was going to enjoy it. No matter what else I did or didn't accomplish at the day spa.

I took Third Street to West Hollywood. The houses along Third look as if they should be on a quiet street, not one of the major east-west roads, and I always imagine shell-shocked homeowners manicuring their front lawns for show, but living their lives in their backyards. In truth, the owners who were bothered by traffic probably sold out a generation ago.

Nirvana was sort of on the West Hollywood/Beverly Hills line, a square brick building with a sizable parking lot to call its own. The building was more attractive from the parking lot side, with a bench and a small rock garden set next to the door, which was in fact the main entrance. I wanted food before my facial, but I figured that any place this tony had to have at least a juice bar, and finding it would give me an opportunity to look around.

The rock garden motif was carried into the foyer, which was a cross between a grotto and the lobby of a small hotel. Even the receptionist's desk was covered with something to make it look like a boulder.

When she discovered it was my first visit, the receptionist insisted on arranging a personal tour with the spa manager. A fiftyish woman in a tailored black pantsuit appeared almost immediately, as if she had only been waiting for such a call.

The woman held out her hand and introduced herself as Tamara. I would have bet that even in high school she was Tamara, never Tammy. Her smooth skin and carefully colored hair, sort of a vanilla caramel, were good advertisements for the spa services, even if her jawline had to have been surgically enhanced. Nobody over forty has a chin that well defined.

"I'm sorry you don't have enough time before your

facial for a mud bath, a swim, and some time in the steam room," Tamara said. "Use of our other facilities is included when you come for a facial or a massage."

That at least partly explained the high cost of facials. Most of their clients must plan to spend the day.

"I was really only counting on a fruit smoothie."

"We can do that," she assured me. "And if you want to come just for a swim and a workout, without personal services, there is only a twenty dollar charge for access to everything. That includes yoga and aerobics, by the way. For two hundred a month, we offer unlimited use of facilities."

For that price, they must offer great yoga.

I wondered why this place wasn't set up to be a club, members only, but I wasn't curious enough to ask. I was already learning more about Nirvana than I really wanted to know.

The pool, mud bath, steam room, sauna, and gym were all on the ground floor. Except for the heavy brown and gray boulder design, they were generic, right down to the smell of disinfectant. The locker room was more attractive than most, but that was the best I could say about it.

I didn't see how many women were in the steam room or the sauna, but neither the pool nor the gym was exactly overflowing with people.

The personal service rooms were on the second floor, as were a nail and hair salon, both full of women being cared for, and the expected juice and sandwich bar. Tamara insisted on comping me the smoothie. We sat down at a small bistro table, the only vacant one. The others were filled with shiny-faced, middle-aged women in designer sweats, all of whom seemed to know Tamara. I was definitely over-dressed in a cotton sweater and loose, flowered skirt.

"What brought you to us?" Tamara asked.

"I haven't had a facial in years, not since I left television." I watched her face express added interest at the thought I might be an actress. "And my skin just hasn't been the same. I found you on the Internet, actually. I was looking for testimonials, not ads, and one for you popped up. Some DJ talking about how she liked to spend her down time. She named several other women who come here regularly, and I figured that if women who can afford to come anywhere come here, the place is offering what I want."

Tamara nodded. "Maria Baca, from KWOW."

"That's right. I was particularly impressed that Jane Browning comes here."

"Well, Jane would," Tamara replied. "Jane is one of the owners. She comes in for a workout almost every afternoon. She could use her home gym, of course, but she thinks it's good for business to use the equipment here."

I was beginning to wish I had worn workout clothes, although I had never liked being in a gym, not even when my paycheck depended on my appearance.

Tamara pulled a pager out of her pocket and glanced at it. I didn't hear it ring, so she must have it set to vibrate unobtrusively.

"Do you have any other questions I can answer?" she asked.

"No, I'm fine," I said. "I'm looking forward to my facial, and I appreciate the smoothie."

"You know which room?"

I waved a slip of paper that the receptionist had given me.

"Stop by on your way out," she said. "Let me know what you think of the facial."

If Tamara gave this much attention to everyone, she couldn't have much time for anything else. And she apparently did. Even though she had been summoned by pager, she stopped by each table to say a word or two before she left the room.

I sat there, finishing my smoothie, and trying to think of a way to approach Jane Browning, one that would make the encounter more successful than my one with Roberta Hill.

I gave up and went to look for my facialist.

She was a short, slight Asian, and she was ready for me, even though I was a few minutes early.

The next hour and a half were blissful. I lay on a padded table in a dimly lit room scented with essential oils of lavender and rosemary while she steamed my face, massaged my hands and feet, placed them in mittens and slippers, cleaned my face, masked my face, massaged my neck and shoulders, and left me thoroughly moisturized. I almost started crying, because I felt cared for, and I couldn't remember the last time I had really felt cared for.

To be fair, of course, I feel cared for when I'm with Michael. But chatting with him isn't relaxing and blissful. The facial was.

At the end, I was so peaceful that I was ready to

forget about Natalie Thorson, go home, and take a nap.

But I couldn't dismiss the image of that pinched, pale face, and the sobbing voice telling me that she couldn't stand it if I stopped helping her, that I was all she had. So I went back to the gym, to see if I could catch a glimpse of Jane Browning.

There still weren't a lot of women in the gym, or at least not a lot using the machines. Only two women were on treadmills, just one pulling weights. No wonder Jane Browning wanted to increase use of the gym. Women were only coming here for the fun stuff.

A handful had moved to the far corner, where mats had been spread. Two were sitting cross-legged, eyes closed. The yoga class was evidently about to begin.

"Now don't you wish you had planned to spend the day?"

Tamara's voice startled me.

"Yes, as a matter of fact, I do," I told her. "Next time I will. And by the way, the facial was marvelous."

"I was certain you'd be pleased," she said.

She stood next to me in a way that made me feel as if I were being ushered out. I had no reason to stay, so I let her guide me to the foyer. In a moment, I was saying good-bye.

Without having found Jane Browning.

I told myself it didn't matter. I would hold on to the peace for as long as I could.

ELEVEN

"IT SOUNDS TO ME as if you've been doing a lot of running around, accomplishing nothing," Michael said, after I had told him about my excursion on Monday. "But if it's making you feel better, go right ahead. I hope you realize, though, how annoyed I am that you went to the theater Sunday without me."

Sitting on the patio of the little restaurant in Los Feliz, taking a break from clients, and eating grilled eggplant and peppers on focaccia was what was really improving my mood.

"I hoped you would understand," I said. "I went without you because I thought you'd interfere with my plan to question Roberta Hill. And you would have. Van might not even have asked me to join them if you had been there."

Michael rolled his eyes to let me know what he thought of my plan to question Roberta Hill.

"I'm not sure any of this is making me feel better, but it's making Natalie feel better," I continued. "And I think I'm on my way to building a case for reasonable doubt where Natalie is concerned. There are certainly other women who lost both money and self-respect because of Craig Thorson. I just have to know a little more about who they are before I talk to Miriam Stern.''

"Who is going to beat you about the head and shoulders for treading in dangerous territory,'' Michael said.

"It's only dangerous if Gary Parkman was murdered,'' I pointed out, "and I don't want to think about that right now.''

"Well, I'm not going to urge you to, especially since you seem to have decided that your life isn't a total disaster after all. Or at least that it isn't this week.''

"But it is a disaster.'' I put my sandwich down. "I've spent the last six years changing my life, leaving one career and creating a new one, and then I went to a play, one play, that made me realize I didn't love anything I had built. All I wanted was to be on stage again. When I was applauding Roberta Hill, I ached to have someone applauding me. I would give up anything but Amy and Mac to be on stage again, just once.''

"The life you've devoted yourself to for the past six years and a play aren't mutually exclusive,'' Michael said. "You can do everything you're doing now—except maybe poke around in a murder—and still do a play. You could join a theater group. You could ask about doing a play at the theater you went to Sunday.''

"But I can't do a play now.''

"No, unfortunately, the universe doesn't move in sync with your whims. You have to find one to audition for first, then be cast, and with your luck Van

Lawrence will be in that one, too." He paused to let me shudder. "Now you have to do the sensible thing, and take care of the life you've built and the clients who pay you money, which you need, since you didn't save a dime when you were making a real salary. Would you really walk away from them?"

"No. I wouldn't." I picked up my sandwich again. "And I did save a dime. That's how I got through graduate school. I just didn't save enough so that I could retire at forty."

Michael flagged down the waitress and asked for a refill on his iced tea.

"I haven't retired. I still have two clients. I simply decided that my time and energy were better spent devoted to Elizabeth's television career. I'm training her to take a single bite of food and then look up at the camera in joy before she takes a second bite." He took a sip of the fresh tea. "Are you sure the desire to be on stage is anything more than a desire to vent emotion on something other than Richard?"

"Oh, God, I've botched it, I've really botched it," I moaned.

"You didn't want it." His voice was totally without compassion. "But more than not wanting a committed relationship with Richard, you don't want to be left for a vacant, untalented child."

"It's not that simple. I do care about Richard, and I wasn't ready to end it."

"That's just it, Faith. I hate to tell you, but I'm on Richard's side on this one. You wanted him to stay until you were ready to end it. He did the right thing."

"*Et tu,*" I grumbled.

"Look," Michael said. "I'm sorry you're upset about Richard. Your ego has been damaged. You want to do a play to get it patched up, but a play isn't available right now. So you have to patch your own ego. And don't blame me."

"My ego has been damaged, and my feelings have been hurt. And you're right, I have to fix it myself." I took a last bite of my sandwich and added, with my mouth full, "But now I have to hurry, or I'll have a client with hurt feelings because I'm late."

"Run along. I'll get the check."

"You don't always have to get the check," I said.

"Think of it as lunch on Elizabeth."

I swallowed the food, tossed my bag over my shoulder, and stood up.

"Give her a kiss for me," I said, leaning over to kiss Michael on the cheek.

He air-kissed mine, a measure designed to let me know he was still annoyed.

I made it from the restaurant to the clinic in record time, but my next client was nevertheless waiting for me.

"I'm sorry," I began, but Mary interrupted me, waving phone messages.

"You have two phone calls, both saying it's important, one from a Miriam Stern and one from an Alicia who didn't leave her last name," she said.

I looked at Betty, my client, who was sitting glumly in the only chair the clinic had room for in the small waiting area. Betty was African-American, homeless after a run of bad luck made worse by bad decisions, and at that moment I had to put her first.

"Come on, Betty," I said. "The phone calls can wait."

The hour went well—after eight months of therapy, Betty was actually beginning to come up with ideas about how to get herself off the street—and then I got a break when my next client didn't show up.

So it was the middle of the afternoon when I returned the calls, first to Miriam Stern. To my surprise, she was there.

"Natalie's son Jimmy has been arrested," she said. "He knifed a man last night, some dispute involving his girlfriend, who's been beaten up pretty badly."

"Alicia's been battered and Jimmy arrested?" I had to repeat it, because it wasn't at all what I had expected. "What happened?"

"Well, we have conflicting stories here. Alicia says the injured man was a drunk who tried to pick her up and then started hitting her when she refused him. She says Jimmy knifed the man because it was the only way to get him to stop. Jimmy, of course, says more or less same thing. The man Jimmy knifed tells a different story." She paused to let that sink in. "He says Jimmy was battering Alicia, and he intervened to save her. The Good Samaritan thing. Then Jimmy knifed him."

"You said Jimmy was arrested. That means the cops believed the other guy."

"The other guy is a forty-year-old in a suit who says he was in the neighborhood seeing an old friend. He drove himself to the hospital, bleeding all over his BMW, and asked them to call the police. And yes, the police believed him," Miriam said.

"I am so sorry to hear this. I have trouble seeing Jimmy as violent, I want you to know that. My first impulse is to believe the kids, that Jimmy struck out to protect Alicia." I was really struggling with the concept of both Jimmy and Natalie in jail.

"You may want to hold off before reaching that conclusion," Miriam said. "In the meantime, the good news is that I might be able to use this to build reasonable doubt where Natalie is concerned. Jimmy used a knife. Maybe he knifed his ex-stepfather, too. I understand there was no love lost between them."

"Oh, Miriam, come on. You really think that would work?" I asked.

"Maybe. I think it enough that I want you to stop asking questions."

"What do you mean?" I asked innocently.

"Natalie told me, Faith. When I let her know about Jimmy, she just went nuts, and she said maybe you could help Jimmy, too. When I asked what she meant, she told me you were helping her by trying to find out who else had a motive to murder her ex-husband. And I want you to stop." Miriam's voice was usually as weightless as a child's. This time, it held authority. She meant those words as an order.

"But I have some ideas," I said plaintively.

"You aren't a police officer, Faith," she said, unmoved by my plaintiveness. "You aren't trained to handle difficult situations, or dangerous people. Let me try to get the police to reopen the case on the basis that Jimmy might have done it."

"But I don't believe he did. I think Craig Thorson may have been involved in some financial stuff, and then there's Gary Parkman's death, the night after I had dinner with him.''

That was the wrong thing to say. I realized that from the silence.

"If you have information about a crime, I need to know what it is," she finally said.

"I don't have anything solid," I replied. "And Gary Parkman's death is probably due to natural causes anyway. I don't have anything that you or the police would take seriously. I just have possibilities."

"You do know that withholding information about a crime could get you in trouble as an accessory after the fact, I hope, and that interfering in a police investigation is against the law." Her voice was getting icier by the minute.

"There is no police investigation, and I'll tell you, I promise, when I have something that could reasonably be called information about a crime." I still sounded plaintive, but I needed her to relent.

"All right, Faith," she said, sighing. "At least stay in touch."

"Okay. I'll call you. And let me know if I can do something to help Jimmy," I said.

"I'll let his attorney know you're available as a character witness. For me to represent him, since I want to use him to create reasonable doubt, would be a conflict of interest."

"Of course."

Miriam gave me the information about Jimmy's attorney, which I quickly scribbled down on a slip of paper and stuck in my bag. I got off the phone as quickly as I could, because I needed to call Alicia.

"Are you all right?" I asked when she answered the phone. "I've talked to Miriam Stern, and I know what happened."

"No, I'm not all right." Her voice sounded muffled, as if she were talking through a towel.

"What can I do to help?"

"Can you come over? I know I wasn't very nice to you yesterday, but you didn't come at a good time." That was as close as Alicia could get to an apology. "Jimmy needs help. Can you come over? Please."

"Yes, I can come over." I'd be helping Alicia, as well as Jimmy, which wasn't something I really wanted to do, but it looked as if this family had become my project. "I'll be there in a few minutes."

I had made the calls on my cell phone, in what was my office for the time I was at the clinic. When I came out, Mary raised her ring-adorned eyebrows and waited for gossip.

"Natalie Thorson's son has been arrested, for an unrelated crime, and I promised his girlfriend, who has been battered, that I'd come over to talk with her," I said.

"Getting this involved with your clients is probably not a good idea, Faith," Mary said. "You know Wendy would be annoyed."

Wendy was Wendy Kormier, the doctor in charge of the clinic.

"You're right, and I'd appreciate it if you wouldn't report me. I'll talk to Wendy when I'm ready."

"And what do I get for being quiet?" Mary asked.

"I'll pay your dental bill when that tongue stud

cracks a front tooth,'' I replied. ''As long as it's only one tooth.''

''Wow! What an offer!'' she giggled, and flashed the tongue stud at me.

''See you Thursday,'' I said, waving good-bye.

About ten minutes later, I was getting out of my car in front of Natalie Thorson's house.

This time, Alicia answered the door immediately. I wasn't prepared for the sight of her face. Her left eye was swollen shut, her mouth was so puffy that her lips didn't meet, and the skin on the left side of her face was almost the color of raw meat.

''My God!'' I gasped. ''Somebody honestly thought that Jimmy might have done that to you?''

''Pretty lame of them isn't it?'' she said.

Now I understood why she sounded as if she were speaking through a towel. Her face was so distorted that it was hard for her to form words.

''Come on in. I needed you to see it. And I wanted you to take the pictures—I need the pictures in case those sick bastards who arrested Jimmy actually take this to trial.'' Alicia stepped back and opened the door.

''Have you seen a doctor?''

''No. I don't need a doctor. I'll be okay. I just need pictures.''

''Why didn't the police take pictures last night?'' I asked.

I followed her into the living room and sat in the same chair I had occupied the last time I was there.

''Because I wouldn't press charges against Jimmy, which is what they wanted me to do,'' she said.

"Oh, hell. I'll take pictures, but I need to hear the whole story."

Alicia nodded and sat down on the sofa, across from me.

"Have you at least put ice on it?" I asked.

"Not yet. I needed pictures first, and I needed them to show how bad it is, and I needed somebody to take them who could get up on the witness stand and have a jury believe. That's you. You dress nice, and Jimmy said you used to be on television. I took aspirin, though." It was so hard for her to form words that I wished I could put off asking for her story.

"Where's the camera?" I asked. "I'll take some shots, then you can talk with ice on your face."

She handed me one of those single-use flash cameras. It had been sitting on the coffee table, right in front of me, but I had been too stunned by her appearance to notice.

I walked around her, shooting from every angle, hoping the pictures would turn out.

"Are there bruises anywhere other than your face?" I asked.

Alicia pulled her T-shirt up so that I could see the redness and the swelling on her chest and stomach. I took more pictures.

"The police really think Jimmy did this to you?" I asked.

"Yeah. Can you believe that? And I would have beat the crap out of him if he'd tried," she said.

I put the camera back on the coffee table, then plopped down into the chair.

"Okay. Now get ice."

I shut my eyes and practiced deep breathing until I heard her come back from the kitchen. I opened my eyes again to see that she had a lumpy towel pressed against the side of her face.

"We needed stuff for breakfast," Alicia began. "Eggs and bread, you know? And the car hasn't been working too good, so I decided to just walk to the grocery store on Sunset."

I knew the store she was talking about, a Latino market, about four blocks away. Quite a hike at night.

"How late was it?" I asked.

"Not too late. Maybe nine o'clock. When I left the store, I walked about a block when this car slowed next to me, and a guy rolled down the window. He said, like, 'Hey, baby,' or something. I ignored him, figuring that when I started up the hill away from Sunset, he'd go away."

"But he followed you?"

"Yeah. I started walking faster, but he didn't take the hint. At the corner he got out of his car and grabbed me." She gestured with her free hand to let me know which corner she meant.

"He grabbed you and hit you?"

"No, he grabbed me and said something, I don't remember what. I yelled at him to get his fucking hands off me, and I kicked his shin. His face got weird, like he just went crazy, and he started hitting me and hitting me." Alicia shut her eyes to keep from being overwhelmed by the memory.

"It's okay," I said. "It's over now, and you're here and you're safe."

Her eyes opened. "I live in L.A., lady. I'm not safe."

Since I had recently moved out of the basin for safety reasons, I couldn't argue. I was sorry I had used the word.

"How did Jimmy get involved?" I asked.

"He says he heard me screaming. I didn't know I was screaming, but he says I was. So he says he came running out, and he saw this guy hitting me, and he started yelling for him to stop, but he didn't stop. So Jimmy pulled out his pocket knife and stabbed him." She shut her eyes again, this time to hold back the tears.

"Jimmy stabbed your attacker with a pocket knife?" Even as I felt concern for Alicia and Jimmy, I wondered how Miriam Stern could possibly draw a connection between Jimmy's pocket knife and the kitchen knife used to stab Craig Thorson. It was one hell of a stretch.

"Yeah. In the side. The guy dropped me, kind of shocked, and he got in his car and drove away. Except he must have seen what house Jimmy came out of or something, because the police knew where to look for us."

"And why exactly did the police arrest Jimmy?" I asked.

"Because the guy said Jimmy was beating me up, and he pulled Jimmy off me and tried to help me up, and that's when Jimmy stabbed him. So the cops didn't really care what we said happened."

Alicia put the towel down on the coffee table. Her face didn't look any better. She was tired and hurt, and I wished I could wave a magic wand and make things right for her. I wish that often, with my clients, but I have no magic wand, so I just keep the dialogue going.

"I asked if I could file a charge against the guy for hitting me," she added, "but the cop said no, he said I was lying to protect Jimmy. So I didn't go with them to the station, and they didn't take pictures of me. I went to bed."

"This is going to be tough," I told her. "If there were no other witnesses, all you can do is find people who will talk to the police about your relationship, say it isn't like Jimmy to be violent."

"Yeah. And who's going to believe us, with his mom in jail for murder?"

"I'm doing the best I can." For the first time that afternoon, I felt a surge of my former annoyance at Alicia returning.

"Who said anything about you?" Alicia asked.

"You're right, I'm sorry." Maybe I was making too heavy an emotional investment in trying to help Natalie. I'd have to watch it. "Do you remember the names of the officers who took Jimmy in?"

Alicia shrugged. I took that to mean she didn't.

"The names will be on the report. I'll stop by the station and see if I can get any more information. It's just about time for the day shift to be coming in to the station and the night shift leaving it, so I may be able to catch the officers before they go out. Is there anything I can do for you before I leave?" I asked.

"I'll be okay."

She didn't look okay.

"Is there anyone you can stay with? Or anyone who can stay with you?" I stood up, ready to leave. "And I still think you ought to see a doctor."

"I'll be okay!" This time she said it so sharply that I backed away, almost falling into the chair.

"Let me know if you think of something that will help either Natalie or Jimmy," I said, backing toward the door. And then I stopped. "Jimmy's last name. I need his last name to talk to the officers. It isn't Thorson, is it?"

"Spencer. Jimmy Spencer."

She didn't get up to see me out.

The Rampart station was only a few blocks away, almost on my path to the freeway. I was turning into the parking lot within five minutes.

I didn't recognize the desk sergeant, a cheerful, young Latino with bright eyes and a flaring mustache. I explained that I was a friend of Jimmy Spencer's family, and asked if I could talk to the officers who had made the arrest.

"Last night?" He tapped a few keys on a computer. "That would have been Page and Davila."

"Are they here? Could you tell them that Faith Cassidy wants to talk to them?" Page and Davila weren't my favorite people, but they might be willing to tell me their side of the story.

"Let me check." He picked up the phone, pushed an extension, said a few words, and hung up. "They'll be right out."

I moved away from the desk so that I could watch the hall. Page appeared almost immediately, followed by Davila, his partner.

CATHERINE DAIN   149

"What can we do for you?" Page asked, swaggering to a stop a little too close for comfort, and giving me his best beady-eyed stare.

"Hi, Faith," Davila said, raising his hand in a half-hearted wave. "I hope you're not organizing another Neighborhood Watch."

I smiled politely at Page and spoke to Davila.

"I've moved out of the neighborhood. No more Neighborhood Watches for me."

"Good," Page said.

"Thanks to you, we've put together a presentation on what Neighborhood Watches are *not* supposed to do," Davila said. "Like have confrontations with armed drug dealers. So why are you here?"

"About the boy you arrested last night, Jimmy Spencer," I said, my face turning red. I didn't need to be reminded that the last time I had tried to help a young man wrongly arrested, the outcome wasn't entirely positive. The young man had been cleared, but not before one of my former neighbors was killed. "He's been accused of battering his girlfriend and knifing a man who tried to intervene."

"Right," Davila said. "Jimmy Spencer. What about him?"

"I just came from talking with Alicia, the battered woman, and I wondered why you believed the other man, not Jimmy and Alicia," I said.

"Are you kidding?" Page asked.

"No. I'm serious."

"The Good Samaritan who got knifed is an adult. He has a family and a profession. It's his word against that of an unemployed college drop-out whose mother is in jail for knifing her ex-husband," Page said, almost snarling at me. "So yeah, we believed him."

Davila shrugged. "He was pretty convincing, Faith."

"But it isn't just Jimmy's word. It's Alicia's word, too."

Page looked at me as if I were a total idiot.

"She didn't say much," Davila said. "And he was standing right there while she said it. In domestic abuse cases, women often want to let their partners off the hook."

"She didn't say much because her mouth was swollen," I argued. "And if you had ever seen the two of them together, you'd know how unlikely it is that he would raise a hand against her, or that she would protect him if he did."

"Tell that to the judge," Page said. "We gotta go."

Davila shrugged. "Sorry, Faith, we can't help you."

I stood aside so that the two men could get past me. Page might have walked right over me if I hadn't.

I retreated to the safety of my car, tired and discouraged and not certain what to do next except go home.

The freeway was a mess. Whether it was worse than usual or I was more tired than usual, it was a mess. By the time I got home, I was ready for a glass of wine and a quiet half hour on the deck to relax.

But first I fed the cats and checked messages.

There were two from clients, and two more. One was from Debbie, saying she had news and asking me either to call before four p.m. or call her in the morning.

The other was the voice that had threatened me before.

"I told you to stop asking questions," the whispery voice said. "Keep it up and you're dead."

I listened to it two more times before I realized that this time it was the last message on the tape. I punched the buttons to call back the last person.

The phone rang and rang, and finally an unfamiliar male voice said, "Hello?"

"Who is this?" I asked.

"This is the pay phone at Halloran's Bar."

"I'm sorry. I must have the wrong number."

TWELVE

ODDLY ENOUGH, discovering that the call came from the pay phone at Halloran's made me feel better. I poured my glass of wine and took it out to the deck, hoping I could sort out what was going on.

The pay phone seemed like some kind of anachronism. The entire population of Halloran's customers would surely have their own cell phones. And use them. So a call would come from a pay phone only if someone was afraid I could somehow trace it back to his cell phone.

If I had turned the tape over to the police, along with the half dozen business cards I had picked up at Halloran's, they could have gotten cell phone records to see if anyone from that group called me. So it must be one of the six, and whoever it was used the pay phone. In the late afternoon. Presumably twice. And maybe someone noticed.

Of course, I could still turn the tape—both tapes—over to the police. But this kind of threat, with no actual violence, wouldn't exactly be a high priority with the overworked LAPD, and there was no telling when they would get around to investigating. Besides, they would no doubt agree with the caller, that I should stop asking questions.

And I couldn't abandon Natalie while she and her son were both in jail, especially not after I had put Debbie on the trail, too.

I decided to wait until morning, after I talked to Debbie, who had information to give me, and who might know something useful about the pay phone at Halloran's, and then I would think about turning the tapes over to the police.

By the time I came to that conclusion, I was calm, and I returned my clients' calls. Both were routine— one had to miss an appointment, one needed to change the time. In truth, most client calls are routine, which is why my cell phone number isn't on my business card, and my answering machine message offers a pager number to use for emergencies. That's my small contribution to stop the cell phone madness that is consuming L.A.

I had a second glass of wine with a salad and some frozen lasagna, one of the so-called gourmet brands that is edible when I can't face cooking for myself and I'm too tired to go out.

I was so tired, in fact, that I went to bed early and slept through the night.

In the morning, I leafed through the Valley section of the *Times,* looking for news of Gary Parkman's autopsy. A two-inch item said preliminary results indicated a heart attack. That further calmed me. If Gary had died of natural causes, no foul play, that strengthened the possibility that he was right about the group at Halloran's, that no one there would seriously threaten to hurt me.

I had only a slight twinge of misgiving over the

rest of the short article, which said that police believed a woman may have been with him that evening, and they were urging anyone with knowledge of her identity to come forward.

It seemed to me that I should consider the possibility that there were two threads here, one concerning Craig Thorson's missing financial assets, which prompted the threat, such as it was, and the other concerning his murder. The threatener and the murderer might be tied only loosely together. I made a second latte to think about that.

I was on my third latte by the time I decided it was late enough that Debbie would be up.

"What did you find out?" I asked.

"David Jacobson is a lot nicer than I expected him to be," she said. "But he's young, and he's just an assistant. Do you really think he could do anything for me? I need to know because he asked me for a date."

"That's your news? About your meeting with Sam's associate?"

"Yes. What did you think it was?"

"I thought you might have something more about Craig Thorson's girlfriends." I felt silly even saying it.

"Oh. Sorry. No. And I'm afraid I'm not going to be able to find out anything more for you." Her voice cooled, then immediately bounced back. "So what do you think about Jacobson?"

"I haven't met him, remember. But off the top of my head, I think that if your interest in him is purely professional, then you should let him know that.'' I felt silly saying that, too.

"That might work in another line of work, Faith, but not this one, and you should know that,'' she said.

"I did. I do. And I also know what kind of trouble you can get into when you lie to people about your interest in them.'' I gave her a moment on that, then moved on. "I got a call from an anonymous caller, from the pay phone at Halloran's. Where is the pay phone, and why does the bar even have one?''

"What do you mean, an anonymous caller?'' Debbie's voice was chilly again.

"Just that. Someone who left a message, no name.''

"How do you know it came from the pay phone?''

"Because I used the feature that lets you call back whoever called you. Somebody picked up the pay phone.''

"From Halloran's,'' Debbie said. "I wondered how he knew.''

"How who knew what?''

"I got a phone call telling me to stop poking around where I didn't belong, or else.''

"Or else what?''

"No name, no specifics. Just creepy enough to freak me out. I didn't realize anybody was aware of what I was doing.''

"I'm sorry. I didn't mean to put you in a position where you might be threatened. I don't think it's serious,'' I said, with what I hoped was a convincing tone.

"Yeah. Still, I don't think I want to eavesdrop any longer," Debbie answered.

"So where is the pay phone?" I prompted.

"In an alcove next to the men's room. I've never seen anybody use it. Everybody always has cell phones."

I sat there trying to decide whether a look at the pay phone was worth a trip to Halloran's. Not that day. Not on a day when I had no other reason to drive over the hill, and when I would have one the next.

"I'll stop by the bar tomorrow," I said. "See what I can find out."

"Pretend we haven't talked," Debbie said.

She hung up. I guess she'd decided to handle David Jacobson on her own.

I had to make one more phone call before I could let the whole thing drop for the day. I had to check in with Alicia, see how she was doing.

The phone rang on, picked up by neither person nor answering machine. I hoped she was all right, but I wasn't driving over there to make certain. Alicia knew how to get hold of me, and for the most part she could take care of herself.

I didn't go out at all, in fact. I had a fairly peaceful day, with relatively peaceful clients. I even slept well that night.

The next morning, Thursday, I was up early so that I could stop by to see Natalie before I went to the clinic.

When I was ready to leave, I tried Natalie's old number again, to check on Alicia.

This time she answered the phone.

"I'm doing okay," she said, in answer to my question. Her voice was still muffled, though, a sign her mouth was still badly swollen. "I can't see too good because of my eye, but well enough to get around. I wasn't here yesterday because I went to see Jimmy. I told him you'd help."

"How's he doing?" I asked, hedging.

"Come on. He's in jail." She waited.

"I don't know that I can help, Alicia. I stopped by to talk with the cops who arrested Jimmy, and they weren't budging. They believed the other guy. If none of your neighbors saw the fight—and you'd be in a better position to look for witnesses than I would— then it comes down to character, and which of you a jury believes." I was not going to get dragged into knocking on doors to look for witnesses. I had done that once, and met Richard in the process. Once was enough.

"They'll believe pictures," she said. "They didn't take pictures of me, but Jimmy told me they did take pictures of his hands. They tried to say that his hands were red and swollen, but they weren't. Did they take pictures of the other guy's hands?"

"I don't know. I'm sure somebody took pictures at the hospital, but I don't know if they would have thought to photograph his hands. And it's too late now," I said.

"Okay." Alicia's voice was dismissive, as if I had somehow failed her.

"I'm going to Sybil Brand to see Natalie," I said. "I'll tell her you saw Jimmy. Can I tell her that he's doing all right?"

"Yeah, I guess. He said his father might make bail for him. Tell her I'll take care of the house until he gets out."

I wasn't certain Natalie would find that reassuring.

With a promise to stay in touch, Alicia hung up.

I grabbed my keys and my bag and walked out of the apartment into a beautiful January day, pausing on the sidewalk to appreciate the clear, blue sky with its few scattered clouds before I retreated to the parking area to get my car.

For a few precious moments I felt cheerful.

Just until I got on the freeway and got caught in a jam where the Hollywood Freeway splits off from the Ventura Freeway.

The traffic cleared a little from Universal City through Hollywood, then jammed again just before the Vermont exit, and stayed jammed until I made it past downtown.

As I crawled through the interchange, I decided I had to get Natalie out of jail, if for no other reason so that I would never have to drive as far east as the San Bernardino Freeway again.

And I wouldn't mind saying a permanent good-bye to the Sybil Brand Institute, either.

I parked in the lot and checked in at the guardhouse, as before. This time the deputy recognized me, but I still had to leave my driver's license. I hurried down the concrete path to the main building, ignoring the women at work in the small rooms along the way.

When the deputy showed Natalie to her spot across from me in the interview area, she plopped down and just stared for a moment before she picked up the

receiver on her side. She looked haggard, eyes unfocused, and I wished I could touch her, hold her hand
for a moment.

"What can you do for Jimmy?" were the first
words out of her mouth.

"Not much, Natalie. I took pictures of Alicia's
bruises and promised I'd testify, but that's it," I told
her. "Alicia is hanging in, although she looks as if
she has to be in pain, and she won't see a doctor. She
said Jimmy's father might agree to bail him out."

"Oh, God, I hope so," she moaned. "This is all
so awful, and it's all my fault. It's the house, it's the
neighborhood. And that girl. Why did he have to get
involved with her in the first place? If I hadn't made
so many mistakes, we'd be living in an area where
he wouldn't have met her and where those things
don't happen."

"First, you can't be sure of that. Bad things happen
anywhere, and young men get involved with women
their mothers don't like everywhere. Second, beating
yourself up isn't going to help," I said. But I understood. I would have been beating myself up if Jimmy
were my kid, jailed for defending his girlfriend, and
I couldn't help because of my own legal problems.

"But beating myself up is all I can do," Natalie
replied. She clenched the fist that wasn't holding the
phone as if she wanted to smack herself. "I can't do
anything to help, and if you can't, oh, God, I hope
his father will."

"Beyond bail, there's not much anyone can do
right now. I've told Alicia to look for witnesses, and
a couple of people testifying that Jimmy wasn't the

kind of guy who would hit her might help, but the cops insisted that the man Jimmy knifed told a credible story." I left unstated the fact that they didn't think Jimmy and Alicia's story was as good.

Natalie leaned forward until her face was close to the plastic shield between us.

"My attorney says she might be able to use Jimmy to create reasonable doubt, try to throw suspicion on Jimmy for Craig's murder," she said. "I've told her that if she tries, I'm jumping up in court and pleading guilty."

"Natalie, you can't do that." I snapped at her, then calmed down. "If you plead guilty, you don't make things better for Jimmy, and you do make things worse for you. I know it's tough on you, being stuck here while Jimmy and Alicia have their own battle with the law, but you have to wait it out. And creating reasonable doubt for a jury, what Miriam Stern is talking about, is a long way from saying there's any evidence that ties Jimmy to Craig's murder. Besides, any trial date is months away, for either you or Jimmy. So please, don't do anything rash, okay?"

"Then you do something, Faith. Please. Do something to get me out of here, without hurting Jimmy."

How did this get back to me?

"I'll do what I can," I told her.

But I didn't know what that was going to be. After ascertaining that she had no more information about her ex-husband's assets, and assuring her that Alicia would be all right—not that Natalie much cared about Alicia—and that I'd check on Jimmy, I said good-bye.

I retraced my way to my car, and thence to the freeway, and back through the interchange, which was just as jammed on the return trip. The traffic was worse than I expected, I sat too long on the freeway, and I was going to be late at the clinic again.

The Silver Lake exit never looked so welcome, the clinic almost lost its aura of despair, and Mary, with her purple hair and assorted studs, seemed sane and healthy compared to Natalie.

"I'm sorry I'm late," I began, but Mary shook her head.

"You look frazzled," she said.

"I am. I don't know how people manage daily commutes," I replied.

"Don't whine, Faith. You're so much luckier than most people, and you know it."

I nodded, chastised, and looked around for Nicole, my eleven o'clock appointment, but she wasn't in the waiting area.

"I have good news and bad news," Mary said. "The good news is that you get a long lunch today. The bad news is that Nicole isn't here, apparently isn't going to be, Luisa asked if you could see her at three instead of one o'clock because she's tied up with the Legal Services people and doesn't know when she'll get loose, and Joanna cancelled her two o'clock. What do you want me to tell Luisa when she calls back?"

I tried to think of something to say that wouldn't sound like whining.

"Tell her I'll see her at three, and I'll see you after lunch," was the best I could do.

I returned to my car and assessed my options. Going home was out. I dismissed the fleeting thought of seeing Richard almost as immediately, knowing it would only end in another scene. The patio restaurant on Hillhurst with Michael was a possibility.

But in response to my cell phone, Michael's machine answered, giving no information other than he was unable to come to the phone, although he really wanted my call, whoever I was. And I didn't want to sit for three hours on the patio alone.

Halloran's was another choice. I had planned to go at the end of the afternoon, but lunch time ought to do as well.

Then I had a better idea—lunch and yoga at Nirvana, and another shot at finding Jane Browning.

I went back into the clinic.

"So soon?" Mary asked, raising her pierced brows.

"Is there a place between here and West Hollywood where I can buy cheap workout clothes?" I asked.

"You mean like thrift store cheap?"

"Well, I don't want to look as if I dressed out of a dumpster." Actually, thrift store was a good idea. The clothes wouldn't look bought for the occasion.

"The Senior Womens League Thrift Store is on your way. You can find designer sweats at bargain prices, some barely worn." Her eyes told me she suspected the sweats would soon go back to the thrift store the same way.

"Of course," I said. "Next to the Tea Room."

"Right, Faith. You can say hello to all your old Hollywood friends while you're there," she said.

The Senior Womens League Tea Room was within walking distance of a couple of television studios, which made it one of those strange places where the lunch crowd was a mix of old money and working actors.

"Just the sweats, Mary, just the sweats. I'm working out for lunch. Really."

She laughed, and I said good-bye to her for the second time.

I drove along Sunset to Fountain, then took Fountain, in that area a stretch of nice little houses and apartment buildings struggling to maintain middle class status, the couple of miles to the Senior Womens League complex.

As often as I had been to the Senior Womens League Tea Room, I had never been to the thrift store. I had gone into the gift shop, which had things like antique silver tea services on consignment, because it was in the same white, colonial building as the tea room. But I'd never wandered around to the other side of the block, where a smaller, tackier building held the thrift store.

When I walked inside, I had to stop for a moment, overwhelmed by the racks of clothing, with hangers packed so tightly there was no wiggle room. Overhead signs identified the clothing by men's, women's, and children's. Two women about my age were working their way down a narrow aisle in the women's section. A third was holding a reluctant preschooler with one hand as she struggled with children's clothes. And an older woman was looking at kitchen equipment, picking up and putting down battered pots and pans.

"I'm looking for sweats," I said to the young Latina at the combination checkout and information counter.

"That way, end of the rack," she said, pointing.

I edged my way past the two women, one of whom turned out to be an actress from a recently cancelled sitcom. We avoided each other's eyes. When I reached the end of the rack, I quickly discovered that Mary was right. For four dollars I could get a bright pink sweat shirt and matching pants from Nordstrom's that looked almost new. Given more choices, I wouldn't have picked that color. But the price was right, the size was right, and I didn't have a lot of time to play around.

Another three dollars got me a pair of serviceable white sneakers, and for one more dollar I picked up a canvas tote, so that I wouldn't be walking into Nirvana carrying a thrift store shopping bag. The thrift store didn't have a dressing room, which made changing there out of the question. I hoped the sweat pants were baggy enough to cover the fact that the black tights I was wearing with my denim skirt and cotton sweater didn't exactly look like gym socks.

Within ten minutes, I was out of the thrift store and on my way to Nirvana.

I pulled into the day spa's parking lot just before noon.

The same young woman was seated at the reception counter, and she smiled as if she remembered me.

"I don't have an appointment for anything today,"

I said, digging my checkbook out of my bag. "I thought I'd stop by for a yoga class."

"One is just starting," she told me. "If you hurry, you won't miss much. Do you need directions?"

"No, thank you. I need a locker, though."

"Just take any one with a key in the lock."

I hurried to the locker room, changed my clothes, and dashed to the gym area as quickly as I could. I slowed down once I was inside, and moved at a fast walk to the far side of the room where six women were sitting cross-legged in front of the yoga instructor.

"Sit down and breathe," the instructor said, smiling. "And take off your shoes."

That meant exposing black tights beneath pink sweats, but I had no choice. I took off the sneakers and set them to one side. Then I sat on a slender plastic mat and breathed.

I had planned to check out the other women, but I found myself caught up in the class, working my body in unexpected ways.

It was only at the end of the class that I looked around to see who else was in the gym.

And I discovered Jane Browning staring at me from a stationary bike.

I got up and walked over, planning to introduce myself, even though I was painfully conscious of my too-pink sweats and wrong black tights. She was wearing a black sleeveless leotard that showed off her sculptured upper arms and blue leg warmers, with a blue sweat band knotted around her head in a way that somehow looked casually perfect.

"You're Fay Cassidy," she said, cutting me off before I could say anything. "You've been asking questions about Craig Thorson. I'd be happy to talk with you, but this isn't the time or place. Would you like to come to my house at, say, five o'clock?"

My jaw dropped almost to the floor before I said yes.

THIRTEEN

SUNSET BOULEVARD, east to west, is a crash course in contemporary L.A. In a way, it's an asphalt artery, beginning slightly to the east of what ought to be the heart of the city, if the city had a heart, at the edge of the old Chinatown. Newer, wealthier, and far less gaudy Asian enclaves lie further to the east, but this is the cinematic Chinatown, and in L.A., the film version is what counts.

Then the road, still narrow and unremarkable, nothing that could justifiably be called a boulevard, passes just north of Olvera Street, the collection of Mexican fast food and souvenir shops that marks the plaza where El Pueblo de la Nuestra Senora la Reina de Los Angeles de Porciuncula was founded. The surrounding residential streets are poor and heavily Hispanic, but the tourist attraction survives.

Through Echo Park and Silver Lake, Sunset remains barely an urban street, clogged with old cars, meandering between minimalls with signs for mercados and botanicas, billboards advertising *cervesa heche en Mexico,* slowing to navigate the narrows carved between bluffs where the houses date back to the boom between the wars—that's World War I and World War II. The concrete retaining walls sport murals painted in a flashy primitive style, with remarkably little graffiti defacing them.

On firmer ground, Sunset begins tossing off the smaller arteries, the side streets that become major thoroughfares of their own as they, too, move west, Santa Monica Boulevard, Fountain Street, Hollywood Boulevard. And here Sunset enters Hollywood, the place where Gloria Swanson was ready for her close-up. But the eastern edge is large hospitals and the Church of Scientology complex, complete with L. Ron Hubbard Drive, dwarfing the old Self-Realization Fellowship building, and most of Sunset through the rest of Hollywood is lined with small shops much like the ones in Echo Park, except that the signs are in English.

There are still television studios on Sunset Boulevard in Hollywood. The few billboards advertise beer and television, although banners hanging from light poles offer images of theaters and museums. The cars are mixed, new and old, limos to the north, clunkers to the south.

And then comes what is left of the Sunset Strip. The Whisky-a-Go-Go sign now says whiskyagogo.com, and even Spago has moved. The murals on the sides of buildings are cool and professional, the Chateau Marmont still overlooks the city, but there is a ghostly effect here.

In West Hollywood, Sunset breaks free. The street becomes wider, the cars newer, the houses larger and farther apart, mansions with landscaped lawns hiding behind trees and fences and small security patrol signs. Then in Beverly Hills there is a wide green median, which disappears shortly before the spires of UCLA rise against the late afternoon sun.

Beyond UCLA, Sunset winds through Brentwood, the transformation from the narrow street with small, battered houses crammed with people on either side to the true boulevard with its lightly populated mansions complete.

Last comes Pacific Palisades, with a bigger, better Self-Realization Fellowship, the Lake Shrine, and finally the ocean. But I didn't have to go that far.

The clinic where I worked was near the east end of Sunset, more or less on the border of Silver Lake and Echo Park. Jane Browning's house was in Mandeville Canyon, off Sunset in Brentwood. So the way to get from one to the other was straight down Sunset, and the only thing that I had to distract me from the traffic was the street itself.

I could have chosen another route, of course. Some Angelenos pride themselves on their knowledge of the surface streets, driving blocks out of their way in an attempt to lessen their involvement in traffic. I think they're kidding themselves. All east-west thoroughfares, and north-south ones too, are jammed in L.A.

Besides, I think somehow that if one could only truly understand Sunset Boulevard, one would understand L.A.

Mandeville Canyon was once so far from the city that it was possible to have a country estate there, complete with horses. Even now, the low wooden fences marking the lower part of the canyon have a rustic quality, and the school with the baseball diamond directly across the street helps to preserve a sense of rural life. But just a few years ago, the current residents screamed—and sued—when a famous director wanted to add a domed riding arena, arguing that he would be cutting down too many trees, and too many people would be involved, adding too much traffic. In a rare move for L.A., the famous director lost the court action.

Jane Browning's house wasn't that high up into the canyon, and in fact was smaller than I anticipated, only one story, white frame, with surrounding trees intact, what would probably be called a ranch-style cottage by her friends. I tried to remember what I had read about her divorce, other than the domestic violence, and whether a larger house had been sold. The lamp attack on her husband was all that stuck in my mind.

I rang the doorbell at ten minutes after five.

A middle-aged Latina, her thick black hair caught at the nape of her neck with a wide barrette, opened the door and stood, staring at me. Her eyes were heavy with crow's feet, her cheeks just beginning to sag into jowls. She was wearing a simple black dress with a scoop neck that looked as if it had been originally bought for someone a little taller and a little thinner.

"I'm Faith Cassidy," I said. "Mrs. Browning is expecting me."

The woman nodded. "You can wait for her on the patio."

She stepped aside so that I could enter, then brushed past me and walked quickly through some kind of living area and through sliding glass doors to a tiled patio.

I barely caught a glimpse of soft white furniture that looked as if no one ever sat in it, two huge vases filled with fresh flowers, and artwork that had a bold, museum-quality look.

The patio had a glass-topped table and four white, wrought iron chairs.

The woman gestured, and I sat, taking a chair that allowed me a view of the backyard, which was narrow, ending against a hillside, but thickly landscaped, with only a small patch of lawn.

She turned on a heat lamp and left without asking whether I wanted anything.

I don't wear a wristwatch, so I couldn't check the time. But it felt like a long wait until Jane Browning opened the sliding doors and stepped through.

Once more, I was conscious of her style. She was wearing loose silk pants and tunic in a champagne color that almost matched her hair, which was cut so that it curled softly around her jaw. She didn't appear to be wearing makeup. Her skin had the glow and firmness that come from regular facials with someone who knows the right acupressure points to massage. For the first time in my life, I felt underdressed for a patio.

"I'm sorry," she began, then stopped and raised her eyebrows. "Didn't Socorro offer you wine?"

"I'm sure she thought I'd prefer waiting until you joined me," I said, as politely as I could.

"I am sorry. I'll be right back," she said.

This time she was back almost immediately, followed by Socorro, who was carrying a silver tray with a bottle of wine in an ice bucket and two glasses.

We watched in silence as Socorro performed her sommelier duties, opening the bottle and offering Jane Browning a sip of the wine before she filled both glasses.

"A votre santé," Jane said, lifting her crystal goblet in my direction.

"Et á votre aussi," I responded, lifting my own.

She nodded. I hoped that didn't mean we were continuing in French. About two more pleasantries would exhaust my ability to speak the language. I sipped the wine.

For the second time in a week, I tasted a truly fine Chardonnay. I considered whether the crystal goblet and the tiled patio made a difference in my perception and took another sip.

"This is a wonderful wine," I said.

"Thank you. Some friends own a winery near Santa Ynez," Jane said. "They've given me several cases, hoping I'll invest so that they can expand their production."

"Do it," I blurted.

She laughed gently. "I'll consider it. Although I'm afraid my only profitable investments right now are the ones my ex-husband's bank holds in a trust. The decisions I've made on my own haven't been as prudent."

I winced at the words "prudent," thinking of Miriam Stern's cautionary words. And I took the mention of investments as my cue to bring up the reason I was there.

"How did you know I was asking questions about Craig Thorson?"

"Roberta Hill and I are friends. We've suffered together through our financial missteps. Some emotional ones as well. And she mentioned that you sought to question her after the play Sunday." Jane paused and looked at me thoughtfully. "Then Tamara mentioned you. She said you asked about my presence at Nirvana. You make an impression, you know."

I wasn't certain whether that was a compliment, so I sidestepped.

"I would have thought a day spa with Nirvana's quality would be a profitable investment," I said.

"Yes, well, that's what I thought, too," she responded, again with a gentle laugh.

"Did Roberta Hill tell you why I was asking questions about Craig Thorson?"

"She said something about a connection to his ex-wife, the one the police have charged with the murder."

"Yes. I think she's innocent."

"Well, she would say that to her friends, wouldn't she?" Jane waved the hand that didn't hold the wine glass, as if dismissing anything Natalie might say.

"We're not exactly friends." I thought about how to phrase it. "I'm a therapist, and I know Natalie Thorson's attorney, and I helped out a bit on another case. I hoped I might be able to help on this one as well."

"My goodness! How fascinating!" Somehow Jane Browning managed to make that come out all right, not like a cliché. "How did you go from being a TV star to being a therapist who helps attorneys? I do remember you from *Coffee Time,* you know, and I'm afraid I have a little trouble seeing you in this new role."

"I wasn't exactly a star. After I was dropped from *Coffee Time,* I had trouble getting work." I didn't feel quite chummy enough to tell her about the cocaine use. "So I had what you might call an early midlife crisis. I went to graduate school and came out a therapist. I met Miriam Stern, Natalie Thorson's attorney, when a neighbor was arrested for something he didn't do."

"You must have been very helpful for her to ask for your aid again," Jane said, leaning forward slightly and topping off my wine glass. "I'd love to hear about your adventures."

"All I did for Miriam then was ask neighbors if they had seen anything." I knew she was trying to control the conversation. I had to turn it around. "I'm doing essentially the same thing this time. I'm just looking for anyone who might know something that would help prove Natalie's innocence."

"Now, Fay—or wait, you prefer Faith now, don't you?" She didn't wait for me to nod. "You're being modest. I think this time you're looking for another suspect."

"The existence of another suspect would certainly help," I answered. "At the moment, though, there isn't one."

"That's good to know. I'm glad you don't suspect me!" Jane said, with the same little laugh. "So if we're not suspects, why did you want to talk to Roberta Hill? And to me? And how did you find us?''

"Well, the murder appeared to be a crime of passion," I said, feeling my face flush. "I thought the way to go was to look for women who might have reason to be angry at Thorson. And a combination of sex and money reasons might be stronger than either one alone. A source suggested that you and Roberta might have more than one reason to be angry at Craig Thorson.''

"'A source?' How mysterious!" She paused to see if I would leap in. When I simply smiled and nodded, she continued. "And how wrong. I hope Roberta set you straight! While it's certainly true that we each made investments that turned out to be worth less than we hoped, it is certainly not true that we were involved, either of us, with Craig Thorson in anything other than a professional capacity.''

I had believed Roberta Hill. I was having a little trouble believing Jane Browning. Something about the wide-eyed sincerity was a little overdone. And on second thought, I had to wonder if Roberta Hill was just a better actress.

"When did you start investing through Craig Thorson? And what led you to him?" I asked.

"I don't remember the year off the top of my head," Jane replied. "Sometime in the mid-nineties. A number of my friends were taking his investment advice, and at the time, he was doing very well for them. Several had the intuitive wisdom to back away before they lost money. A few of us didn't.''

"The rumor that he slept with his female clients is

pretty widespread. Do you know how much of it is true?'' I asked.

"Oh, my dear, no,'' she said, shaking her head and laughing. "Craig was charming, of course, and while it's quite possible that one or two of his clients succumbed to that charm, no one confided in me about it. I'm always the last one to hear the dirt.''

Now I really didn't believe her.

"Does that mean you have no idea who could have been so angry at Craig Thorson that she picked up a kitchen knife and stabbed him?'' I looked straight into her eyes as I asked, hoping she would blink.

She didn't.

"Well, my dear, really, don't you think his ex-wife is the most likely suspect?'' she countered. "If what you've been told is true, then he was betraying her trust even as he was losing her money. What better reason for murder?''

"I can't think of one,'' I answered. "I just don't think the person who picked up the knife was Natalie.''

"Then I certainly wish you well in your attempt to help her,'' Jane said, leaning back in her chair.

At that moment, Socorro walked out onto the patio and whispered something to Jane that I couldn't hear. The timing was so perfect that I had to wonder whether this hadn't been prearranged, whether Jane had given some kind of signal.

I knew pretty much what her next words were going to be.

"My attorney is on the line, saying it's important that we talk right now.'' She softened them with a smile. "I don't know what she wants, so I don't know how long I'll be. I think it might be better if we said good-bye, at least for the time being. I would, of course, be delighted to talk with you again sometime."

"And, of course, you'll call me if you think of anything that might cast suspicion on someone other than Natalie," I said, matching her smile.

"Of course. Now, if you'll excuse me..." She stood and held out her hand.

I hated leaving the wine.

I shook Jane's hand briefly and watched her walk through a second glass door, one that led to a bedroom. I caught a glimpse of white bedspread when she turned on the light.

Socorro was waiting to show me out. I followed her to the front door in silence.

She shut it behind me without saying good-bye.

Once on the street, I looked up at the evening sky. Mandeville Canyon was far enough from the city itself that there was no telltale haze. I suspected that one could even see stars here, the real ones, on clear nights. The last time I had seen the stars in the night sky was on a vacation to Maui.

I wondered if Jane Browning appreciated how lucky she was. I doubted it.

The peaceful setting—and the glass of Chardonnay—almost made the hour-plus drive down Sunset worthwhile. Almost. Jane had wanted to charm me, or intimidate me, or something, but she hadn't planned to give me information. On that part, she succeeded.

I wanted another glass of wine, and I didn't feel like fighting the traffic on the San Diego Freeway over the hill to Sherman Oaks. Besides, I was feeling spoiled, and I wanted something a little better than my house wine. My other choice was to do what I had originally planned, to check out the pay phone at Halloran's. That meant fighting the traffic on Wilshire Boulevard. But it meant a glass of a drinkable Chardonnay, and I could get something to eat there, maybe a veggie burger. Even faux Irish pubs in L.A. served veggie burgers these days.

Driving back along Sunset, I was going against the major flow of traffic for a while, but by the time I hit the Strip, all lanes were stop and go. On La Brea, I dropped down to Wilshire, then turned left to Halloran's.

At least the parking god was still smiling on me. I found a spot a few doors down, so I didn't need to spring for the parking garage.

The pub was close to full, as it had been the first time I was there. And again, the clientele was mostly men in three-piece suits. The few women that I could see, except for Debbie, were dressed as conservatively as the men. Debbie, who was wearing a T-shirt and jeans that appeared only slightly more out of place than my cotton sweater and denim skirt, didn't acknowledge my presence.

One of the tables held Jason Kohl and four younger men who were either the same as his drinking buddies on my earlier visit or their clones. Kohl had his jacket off and his shirt sleeves rolled up, as if he might be doing some heavy-duty drinking. I ignored them and looked for a stool at the bar.

This time I wasn't startled when Bill the bartender slapped his hands on the bar in front of me.

"Chardonnay," I said. "Something pretty good. And can I get a veggie burger here at the bar?"

"Fries or cottage cheese?" he asked, nodding.

"Fries." I've always thought the people who order cottage cheese with a burger must be on a delusionary diet, like the ones who order diet soda. Fast food is fat food, and if you're going to eat it, admit it.

Bill placed my glass of Chardonnay on a napkin.

"Your veggie burger will be right up," he said.

"I don't suppose you'd notice if somebody in here used the pay phone," I said.

"What's the matter, cell phone dead?"

"No, I don't need to use it. But somebody called me from the pay phone here, and didn't leave a name. I wondered if you have any idea who he could be."

"None at all," he said over his shoulder as he moved away.

I took a sip of the Chardonnay, which turned out to be the same one he had served the last time I was there. Not bad, but a real comedown after the glass Jane Browning had poured. I put it down and covered it with my napkin, to let anybody interested in the bar stool know the spot was taken, and began to work my way to the back of the pub, where a discreet sign said Restrooms.

Debbie almost ran into me with her tray, pretending I didn't exist.

Jason Kohl and the gang of four also ignored my

presence. I found that a little odd, considering the fuss
Jason had made when he met me.

The restrooms were in a narrow, dimly lit hallway
leading to a door with a neon exit sign above it. The
pay phone was right next to the men's room, just as
Debbie had said. It had a shelf underneath and wings
to either side, so someone using it had a modicum of
privacy. And could easily remain anonymous. If anyone came back here to use either the men's or
women's room while the call was being made, only
the back of a coat would be visible.

This was clearly a wasted trip, except for the wine,
and I was ready for the veggie burger.

I was about to return to the main room when a
man's arm slammed across my chest, knocking the
wind out of me.

"Goddamn it," a voice whispered in my ear.
"Don't make me kill you."

FOURTEEN

I TRIED TO SUMMON enough breath to scream, but it wasn't there.

"Don't do this, Jason," was all I managed to gasp out.

I couldn't be certain it was Jason Kohl, but sometimes, as they tell you on the game shows, your first impulse is the right one. Besides, the beefy arm across my chest wasn't wearing a coat.

The arm wavered and shifted. Then with both hands on my shoulders, he shoved me against the wall, forehead first, and let me go.

My head collided with the wall so sharply that for a moment I could only see little flashing lights. I thought vaguely that they didn't really look like stars, more like white fireworks, and then they began to subside.

I held on to the wings beside the phone until I began to feel steady again. Then I eased my way into the ladies room to check my face in the mirror.

About a third of my forehead was bright red. I soaked a paper towel in cold water and pressed it gently to the spot. I closed my eyes to concentrate. I had to decide what my next step would be before I went back to the bar, and I didn't like any of my choices.

Confronting Jason was the most attractive choice on the level of fantasy, and I knew I wasn't going to do it. In reality, the boys at the table wouldn't believe me, and I would feel stupid as well as hurt. In fact, I already felt stupid as well as hurt.

So I had to either sit at the bar and eat my veggie burger and drink my wine as if nothing had happened, or I had to get the sandwich packed to go, leave my wine, and slink away.

"Are you all right?"

I turned, startled, and realized that Debbie had stuck her head inside the door that led to the hall.

"Your sandwich is ready," she added.

"Just a headache," I said. "I don't suppose you have any aspirin."

"This is a bar. Of course we have aspirin. Do you want me to bring you the bottle?"

"No, that's okay. I'll be out in a minute."

She nodded, and her head disappeared behind the door.

That decided it. I would take the aspirin, eat the veggie burger, and see what effect my bluff had on Jason Kohl.

I tossed the paper towel in the trash and tried to fluff out my hair so that it would cover the redness on my forehead. The result was that I looked a little drunk. I pulled a brush out of my purse and tried again. Not much better, but it would have to do.

I took a deep breath and left the ladies room, prepared to stare down Jason Kohl.

And was promptly disappointed. He and his buddies had left. Debbie was clearing the empty glasses from their table.

When I had threaded my way through the room to my bar stool, I found that she had left the aspirin bottle and a glass of water next to the plate with the veggie burger and fries. I swallowed two tablets with half of the water and shut my eyes, willing the pain-killer to take immediate effect.

Then I attacked the food. I had been hungry to start with, and the stress had magnified the need for sustenance. I had to force my body to slow down and process the sandwich. And the fries. They were greasy and salty, but good.

I was about halfway done when Debbie paused beside me, tray in hand.

"Feeling better?" she asked.

"Much, thank you. By the way, I don't suppose you noticed whether Jason Kohl went to the men's room before he left." I was sure it was Jason who had grabbed me, but since all I really had to go on was a whispered voice and a sleeveless arm, I wanted some corroboration.

Debbie rolled her eyes. "No idea."

And then she was off again. I knew there was no point in trying to get anything more out of her.

When Bill came over to offer a refill on the wine, I shook my head, causing a twinge of pain.

"Jason Kohl and his friends left early," I said.

"Memorial service for a drinking buddy tomorrow," he answered. "Nobody felt like being social tonight."

"Gary Parkman? Where is it?"

"Toluca Lake. Ten a.m." He gave me the name of the church and walked away.

Did I want to go? Not really. I would sleep on it and decide in the morning. But if I intended to keep asking questions, despite my bashed forehead, Gary Parkman's memorial would be a better spot than most.

I felt a pang of guilt that I couldn't raise a little sadness about his death. Every death diminishes me, and all that. But I was too tired to care much about anything.

And too discouraged. The bashed forehead was the only thing I had to show for my efforts to date.

The attack, such as it was, would have dissuaded me more if I believed Jason Kohl was Craig's killer and might be planning to seriously hurt me. But I just didn't believe his threats. If they were real, if he were really working his way up to murder, he would have done something other than manhandle me briefly in a hall where anybody could have walked in on us.

Jason Kohl wasn't the killer. Or at least I didn't think he was. But he was desperate about something, worried that something might come to light. And there was nothing I could do about it just then.

So I finished my sandwich and wine, paid my tab, and left.

My drive home was slow and smooth, the first time all day something had felt slow and smooth.

I fed the cats, returned phone calls that had nothing to do with Natalie Thorson, and went to bed early.

My headache returned in the middle of the night,

and it took a while for two more aspirin tablets to kick in. I lay there in bed and thought about giving up the project. No more questions for anyone about anything.

Even as I thought about it, I knew I wouldn't stop. I had started this process, whatever it was, I had promised Natalie I would do my best to help, and the monster called Compulsion to Finish What You Start had taken over. The only way I knew to cope with the monster was to give it what it wanted.

In the morning, I even felt a little better.

I had fixed my first latte and was examining my forehead in the bathroom mirror, wishing I had a heavier foundation to cover the slight discoloration, when the phone rang.

"Jimmy's out of jail," Alicia said. She sounded healthier, but her voice was still a little mushy. "His father bailed him out. And he wants to talk to you."

"I would be happy to talk with him, too, but there's no way I can drive to Silver Lake today," I told her. "He'll have to wait until tomorrow. How's he doing? And how are you doing?"

"We're both okay. What time tomorrow?"

"Either ten in the morning or four thirty in the afternoon. Your choice." I could think of no reason to see Natalie, and seeing Jimmy in her time slot sounded right.

I heard mumbling in the background as Alicia conferred with Jimmy.

"Come in the morning," she said. And hung up.

"Have a nice day," I said to the dead phone.

The call had distracted me for just long enough that

I had to hurry getting ready for Gary Parkman's memorial service.

No more fussing over my forehead. I slapped some makeup on, and once again brushed my hair in a way that I hoped would camouflage the spot.

I rummaged in the closet for something appropriate to wear, but the nearest outfit for a funeral I owned was the dark green pantsuit I had worn the night I met Parkman for dinner. I thought fleetingly that some Cosmic Jokester might chuckle at the synchronicity, but I put it on anyway.

The telephone book yielded an address for the church. I had a sense of where it was and decided that I didn't need to consult a map. I grabbed my purse and keys and left.

The freeway was clear, all the way to Toluca Lake, an upscale suburb with mansions and landscaped grounds not all that different from Beverly Hills, but flatter. Once upon a time, Toluca Lake had seemed a long way outside the city. Now it was right next door to major Industry centers. Hollywood had moved to the Valley, and was now called Burbank.

The church was where I thought it was, and I arrived there fifteen minutes before the service was due to begin.

Everything felt wrong. The church was one of those white frame structures with steeple and bell on an expanse of green lawn that roused memories of rural childhoods, even for those of us born and raised in the city. It cried out for parishioners to approach with peace in their hearts.

But the people walking up to the front door, mostly

men, with a sprinkling of women, all looked as if they were taking time out from a busy work schedule, an hour at most, and would head back as soon as they politely could. My dark green suit fit right in. The only people wearing black were the ones for whom it was daily dress.

I looked for signs of grief, but the closest anyone came to that was a kind of hangover pallor that marked the faces of two of the boys from Halloran's.

I put my head down, not wanting to attract their attention, and slipped into the ragged line moving toward the chapel.

The inside of the church was quiet except for the muted sounds of an organ playing something of Bach's that I couldn't identify offhand. The light was as muted as the sound, filtered through a stained glass representation of Jesus with a halo, hands held up to bless the congregation. I wondered if church architects learned in school how to create that kind of atmosphere, one that seemed to absorb everything that entered it.

I took a seat in the last pew, off to one side, where I could watch the mourners. I was mildly surprised to discover Roberta Hill and Jane Browning among them, whispering to each other, about third row center.

I was more surprised to see Tamara, the spa manager, on Jane's other side.

The person I had expected to see—Jason Kohl—hurried in at the last minute. He moved down the other side of the chapel and took a seat next to Tamara, exchanging quiet greetings with the three women.

Since this was a memorial service, there was no coffin around. I was glad that I wouldn't have to make a decision about viewing the body. Even though he had apparently died of natural causes—I was listening to the whispers of the people around me, all of whom had known him better than I had, and no one was saying anything to the contrary—I had no desire to pay last respects.

So what did I expect to accomplish? I still wasn't sure. But I knew that police detectives went to funerals to see if the killer showed up and gave himself (or herself) away. I hadn't attended Craig Thorson's funeral. I wasn't even sure when it had been held, because I hadn't yet been paying attention to the case. So this was as close as I could get. And I had a gut feeling that whoever murdered Craig Thorson was here.

Even Bill, the bartender, was here, two rows in front of me. I spotted him when he looked around restlessly.

A minister finally stepped up to the altar about ten minutes after ten. After an opening prayer and a few carefully chosen words about death as an end of the old and beginning of the new that would have gone over better with a different audience, he explained that he hadn't known Parkman, and was therefore turning the service over to those who had.

The first one up was Gary Parkman's son, a thirty-something young man who had a lot of trouble getting the words out. The underlying message was that he was struggling to get past an estrangement with his dead father that he was now going to have to heal on his own. I hoped he had sense enough to get help.

The next one up was Jason Kohl.

I closed my eyes to listen to his voice, trying to determine whether he was indeed the man threatening me, both over the phone and in Halloran's hallway.

I thought he was. I just couldn't be certain. But if it wasn't Jason, who was it?

A cell phone began ringing, ending my meditation, such as it was. I opened my eyes and took another look around the chapel.

The owner of the phone must have had the rare grace to shut it off, because I didn't see anyone talking.

Slowly, what Jason Kohl was saying began to penetrate. He and Gary Parkman had actually been friends, as well as golfing partners and drinking buddies. Whatever was going on, and despite my initial impression, it was clear that Jason was genuinely grieving.

Maybe in the sunlight outside the church I could find a way to talk with him—prudently, of course.

Several other friends and colleagues spoke after Jason, but none were people I had encountered at Halloran's. As each talked about what a nice guy Parkman had been, I found myself beginning to like him better dead than alive. Not that I had expected anyone at the memorial service to speak ill of the dead, or even realistically.

After an hour or so of the short speeches, the minister returned. He introduced a young man who sang

"The Impossible Dream" to organ accompaniment. I wondered if it had really been Parkman's favorite song. It didn't seem to fit with the man I met.

And that was essentially it. The minister said a few words of closing, and a breath of relief swept through the chapel. Everybody could now go back to work.

I stayed in the pew, planning to work my way out right behind Jason Kohl, once he got to the rear of the chapel.

But when I stood up and moved to the aisle, Bill the bartender was blocking my path, still looking restlessly around.

"Who's missing?" I asked, trying to edge my way around him.

"Debbie," he answered. "You seen her?"

"Not today," I responded.

"Could you check the ladies room for me? See if she got sick or something?"

"She was here?"

"Yeah," he nodded. "We were going to sit together, but she wanted to take a pee before the service started. She never came back."

Checking for Debbie would mess with my plan to confront Jason Kohl, but I didn't see how I could reasonably refuse.

I squeezed my way through the bottleneck at the chapel door, Bill following. A discreet sign at one end of the foyer pointed toward the restrooms.

Several other women were headed in the same direction, and I decided not to push to the front of the pack. The ladies room contained three stalls, and it didn't take long to realize that women were only coming out of two of them.

I banged on the door of the third.

"Hello! Debbie?"

No answer.

The two women in line to use the stalls, the one washing her hands, and the one fixing her makeup all glanced at me, then looked away, ignoring the impropriety as I got down on my knees to peer under the door.

I didn't really expect to find Debbie in there.

But she was. She was sitting there, fully clothed, head propped against the wall, eyes wide open and staring.

The women paid attention when I screamed.

FIFTEEN

THE MINISTER TOOK CHARGE of the situation. Or at least I think he did. Somehow he showed up in the ladies room, and then he got all of us out. I heard him urging the people who were trying to leave the church to return to the chapel and wait for the police. I'm not certain how many of them did.

Shelly, the woman who had been fixing her make-up, was deputized to keep the five of us who had been in the ladies room when I started screaming together in the minister's office. There wasn't much space, and nobody wanted to sit in the minister's chair behind the desk, so Shelly and I took the two straight leather-back chairs in front of the desk and the other three women crowded onto the overstuffed sofa.

Shelly turned her chair so that she could see all of us at once, prepared in case one of us got hysterical, or try to run. I half-turned mine, leaving it so that I could still see out of the window that took up most of the wall behind the desk. Despite the minister's exhortation to stay, a line of cars was streaming out of the lot.

We sat uncomfortably in silence, until Shelly asked, "Who was she?"

"A waitress at Halloran's," I said. "And an actress."

"Halloran's? Half the men here must have known her," one of the women on the couch said.

"But she was killed in the ladies room," I blurted.

That took us back to silence.

Two of the women on the couch whispered something about a meeting, and one of them pulled out a cell phone and walked over to the window, as close to privacy as she could get. I still overheard her half of the call. She didn't mention the word "murder" when she said she'd have to cancel.

The police arrived unannounced, no sirens, and blocked the exit from the lot. The ambulance arrived quietly as well, parking in the red zone in front of the church. It took another five minutes before the minister opened the door to introduce the two men who would interview us, Detectives Godines and Belson.

"Which of you found the body?" asked Godines, a tall, clean-shaven Latino with a lean face and round, dark eyes. He was wearing a fringed vest over his tan shirt and jeans. A guy who knew he was impressive without dressing for success.

I raised my hand, and he nodded. He conferred briefly with Belson and the minister, who then ushered the other four women out of the room, leaving Godines alone with me.

Godines had no problem taking the seat behind the desk.

"I didn't catch your name," he said, locking my eyes with his.

"Faith Cassidy."

He pulled out a notebook, flipped it open, and quickly scribbled a few words, something more than my name.

"And you went into the ladies room specifically to look for the victim?"

"Yes. Her friend Bill asked me to. The bartender at Halloran's. I don't know his last name. Or hers." I felt my face start to flush. I had only said a few sentences, and I already felt like an idiot. "How did she die?"

"Blow to the back of the head. How did you meet her?"

Prompted by Godines, I stumbled through an explanation of how I knew Debbie, how I knew Bill, how I knew Gary Parkman, and what I was doing at his memorial service. Sort of, anyway. I was trying to figure out how to bring up the connection to Craig Thorson's murder, and the threats Debbie and I had both received, when it really hit me.

I hadn't taken the threats seriously, hadn't thought I was in trouble, or Debbie was in danger. But Debbie had been murdered. Blow to the back of the head.

"Oh, God," I moaned, and I dropped my face into my hands.

Godines waited until I lifted it up again before he asked, "What is it that you don't want to tell me?"

"That I got her into this," I said, poised for his judgment.

No clap of thunder, no lightning strike. He simply nodded and waited.

Godines would have made a great therapist. I looked into his deep eyes and spilled all. He somehow took notes without ever breaking the connection between us.

When I finally stopped talking, he said, "And you still have the audio cassette from your answering machine? The one with the threat?"

"I still have both of the cassettes. I can give them to you this afternoon."

He nodded and made a note. "Are you willing to lodge a complaint against Jason Kohl for attacking you in the bar last night?"

"I can't," I said. "I can't be certain he was the one."

"If he is the one, you may be in danger."

"But the murderer has to be a woman," I argued. "If Jason Kohl had gone into the ladies room, someone would have seen him."

Godines just looked at me.

"You think I'm in trouble either way, don't you?" I asked.

"I'll have an officer drive you home to pick up the cassettes," he said, dodging my question. "Is there someone you can stay with for the next few days?"

"No. I don't want to leave my apartment. And my cats." I wanted to tell him I could drive my own car, but I was feeling shaky enough that I decided I'd rather ride.

"Then is there someone who could stay with you?"

"I'll have to think about that." My choice would have been Richard just a few days earlier. Michael wouldn't want to leave his own cat. And I couldn't come up with anyone else I was close enough to, no one I could ask this kind of favor.

"Think about it seriously," Godines said. "Being alone may not be a good idea right now."

"You really do think I'm in danger." I couldn't feel a sense of danger. All I could feel was queasiness and guilt.

"I think you may be in danger if Debra Pierce's murder was connected to the inquiries about Craig Thorson. Right now, that's a big if. But I'd rather you didn't take any chances. And that means no more questions about Thorson. Of anyone." His voice was quiet but firm, a parent talking to a child.

"Okay," I said meekly. I was somehow a little relieved to know Debbie's last name.

Godines stood up.

"I'll get that officer now," he said.

In fact he got two uniformed officers, a woman to drive my car and a man to follow in a black-and-white.

The woman had dark hair knotted at the back of her head, just under the edge of her officer's cap, no makeup, and a cop's attitude that softened so much once we were alone in the car that I wondered if I had been set up, whether Godines thought I might have more to say.

But I didn't. And I couldn't help asking her a question.

"Do you know what Debbie was hit with?" I asked.

"Afraid not," she answered. "Tell me where to get off the freeway."

I gave her directions to the apartment building.

Her partner stayed discreetly in the car while she walked up the stairs with me.

Amy and Mac were waiting right inside the door, but they backed off when they saw I wasn't alone.

"Hi, babies," I said.

The officer started to follow me in, then stood to one side as if she didn't like cats.

"Sorry. Allergies," she said, when I looked at her.

"I'll get the cassettes."

It only took me a moment to retrieve them. I handed the cassettes to her, and she looked at me with the stern expression a teacher might have for a truant.

"Are you sure you don't want me to stay until you can find a friend to come over?" she asked. "Or at least until you get someone on the phone?"

"No, thank you. I'll be fine," I answered.

She nodded and left.

All of a sudden I really felt alone. And on the edge of panic.

I fixed myself a latte, figuring I might as well add caffeine to the adrenaline rush, then sat down to make phone calls.

The first three were to the clients I was expecting that afternoon. Cancelling at the last moment wasn't exactly professional, but none of them had pressing problems, and I wasn't sure I could stay focused while they talked. I was afraid I'd keep flashing on Debbie's dead body.

I got one answering machine and two actual clients, one who rescheduled cheerfully without asking for an explanation, bless her heart, and another who didn't think I deserved a personal emergency. I wouldn't let her talk me out of it.

Then I called Richard.

"Richard, pick up," I said, after listening to the message and waiting for the beep. "I need help. Please."

I had to wait a very long ten seconds or so before the receiver clicked and Richard said, "What, Faith?"

"I discovered a dead body this morning, and the detective thinks I may be in danger. Is there any way you could stay with me tonight?" I asked.

"Oh, God, Faith. Please tell me this is a joke."

"Not a joke."

Long silence. Longer than ten seconds. I was afraid he was going to hang up on me.

"Richard?" I added, just to make sure he was still there.

"No," he said, sighing. "No, I will not stay with you tonight. I will not drop everything and come running because you have gotten yourself into trouble. In case you've forgotten, we're not exactly getting along very well. I even thought we had stopped sleeping together. I would have described us as broken up. On top of that, I'm taking care of my own life right now. I'm getting work together for a gallery show, remember that? So you'll have to get someone else to hold your hand."

"You don't believe I was threatened, do you?" I started to channel my fear into anger. It felt better that way.

"I do believe it. I just don't believe I can do anything about it. I also believe you'll take care of whatever-it-is just fine without me.''

"I'm not asking you to do anything about the threat. I'm only asking you to help me cope with it," I argued.

"Only," he repeated. "Only asking me to help you cope. You'll cope just fine with the threat, Faith. Really you will. This crisis and the next one, too. And the one after that."

"You don't even care what happened, do you?" I asked, feeling the nervous energy evaporate from my body.

"I'm not insensitive," he said, flaring for a moment, then calming down again, as if he had decided in advance what the best way to handle me was. "I'm sorry you found a dead body, sorrier for the dead person than for you, in fact, and I'm sure it's a good story. But no, I don't want to hear it."

"Frankly, my dear, I don't give a damn," I said.

"Somebody said that in a movie. But life isn't a movie, and I don't want to live mine as if it were. Okay?"

"No, this isn't okay." I could feel tears in my eyes, and I didn't want to cry. "I shouldn't have called."

"Probably not."

I managed to squeak out a good-bye before I hung up.

That left nobody to call but Michael.

"I discovered a dead body this morning," I began for the second time. But that was as far as I got before I started crying.

"Are you home?" Michael asked.

"Yes," I sobbed.

"I'll be over with food in about half an hour."

"Could you bring your jammies, too?" I asked. "The detective thinks I may be in danger, and I shouldn't stay here alone."

He only paused for an instant.

"I'll stay at your place tonight," he said. "Partly because I don't want to feel guilty over your untimely demise if the detective turns out to be right and partly because I don't think you ought to drive when you're hysterical, so I can't ask you to come here. But if you still need company tomorrow night, then you have to sleep over here."

"Deal," I told him.

I hung up the phone feeling so much less stressed that I could finally get in touch with my hunger. I had eaten a bran muffin with my second latte of the morning, but that had been a long time earlier. And whatever Michael brought would be better than anything I could fix for myself.

I thought about another latte, but enough caffeine was enough. I poured myself a glass of mineral water instead and took it out to the deck. Amy slipped past as I opened the sliding glass door, and she and Mac both made it to the chaise before me.

I gently repositioned Mac so that there was room for me to sit. I closed my eyes and tried to focus on what I could do next.

Nothing came to me except the image of Debbie's body propped on the toilet. When I shut that out, all I could think of was Michael coming with food.

Maybe I was going to have to keep my promise to Detective Godines. No more questions.

Michael's knock at the door jolted me out of my slump.

"I brought pizza because it was fast," he said. "With green peppers, mushrooms, and olives. Now tell me what happened."

I could smell the pizza. My favorite toppings.

"You have to wait until I eat a little bit," I told him. "And thank you for coming."

It took about half a slice before I could slow down enough to tell him about the memorial service for Gary Parkman, Debbie Pierce's murder, and the session with Detective Godines. I had to back up to fill in my meeting with Jane Browning and my trip to Halloran's. And for the second time that day, I had to confess to withholding information about the threats.

"You were threatened twice over the phone? And that didn't faze you?" Michael asked.

"Well, it fazed me. But the threat came from somebody at Halloran's, and Gary Parkman thought nobody there would threaten me seriously, and he seemed to be involved in this whole thing," I answered.

"Faith, Gary Parkman is dead, remember?"

"But his death is apparently from natural causes," I argued. "There haven't been any rumors of foul play, or at least not any that I could pick up at the memorial service."

Michael glared at me. "Whether Parkman's heart attack was natural or induced, Craig Thorson and

Debbie Pierce were both murdered, and Debbie apparently received threats from the same person who threatened you. And somebody roughed you up. You have to take the threats seriously. You should have done that from the beginning.''

''Yes, but Craig and Debbie were both murdered by women. Or at least it looks that way. And a man threatened me. I think Jason Kohl, who doesn't seem murderous. And he didn't rough me up very seriously.''

''Fine. Who does seem murderous?''

''Oh, God, Michael. I wish I knew.'' Tears began welling up in my eyes again, and I put my pizza slice down to wipe them away.

''I know this has hit you hard.'' He reached out to take the hand that wasn't wiping tears. ''I just wish you had seen the danger a little earlier.''

''So do I. But Debbie took the threat seriously, and she's dead anyway. And then on top of everything, Richard rejected me again.''

''What? Richard? When?''

''Just before I called you, I called him,'' I sobbed. ''He didn't even want to hear about it.''

''I'll put my pique at being your second choice aside for the moment,'' Michael said. ''Did you really expect him to come rushing over to save you?''

''He might have. More important, I wanted him to. And you have to excuse me for a moment.'' My mascara was running into my eyes, and I needed to rinse my face before I could continue.

I took my time in the bathroom, taking all my makeup off, waiting until I had regained some composure before I returned to the conversation with Michael.

"What do you think I should do now?" I asked, when I sat back down at the table.

"You're asking me? Really?"

"Yes. I need to hear what somebody else thinks. I need to eat, too. You talk while I eat."

"I think you should keep your door locked when you're here, stay away from Halloran's, and do what you promised the detective you'd do—stop asking questions. And you knew I'd say that." Michael sat back and crossed his arms, daring me to contradict him.

"You left out what I should say to Natalie," I said around a mouthful of pizza.

"The truth. That somebody else was murdered, you've told the police you think the two are connected, and that's all you can do." He said it so calmly that I had to consider whether he was right.

"I'll think about it. I'll sleep on it tonight and go see Natalie in the morning. I'll see how it goes."

"Fine. And just to make certain, I have to ask you something else. You do know, don't you, that Debbie Pierce being murdered is more important than Richard rejecting you?"

I glared at him. "Yes, of course I know that. It was the insult on top of the injury, though, that made me cry."

"Okay. As long as you're clear on that. And now we have to decide what to do about the afternoon and evening, since I've promised to keep you company while you're sleeping on your next step."

"Movies," I told him. "Movies and wine. I have the wine. And you have to go to the video store, because I'm not ready to go out. Classic mysteries would be good, especially ones with Robert Mitchum."

"I'm off. Where's the nearest Blockbuster?"

I gave him directions and let him out, locking the door behind him. I would have done that anyway, but I was feeling the need for a locked door more than usual.

And I was glad he was coming back. I couldn't have made it through twenty-four hours alone.

He was back in less than an hour, just time enough for my panic to rise, not time enough for it to overwhelm me.

We had our own *film noir* festival, starting with *Out of the Past,* moving on to *Macao,* leaving Robert Mitchum long enough for *The Maltese Falcon* and *Gilda,* and coming back to him for *Farewell, My Lovely* and *The Night of the Hunter.*

Watching all the murder and mayhem was a little creepy, in one way, because of what was going on in my life. In another way, though, it was comforting. Whatever happened in any movie, Robert Mitchum lived to be in the next one. I had to hold on to the idea that there would always be a next movie.

Between *The Maltese Falcon* and *Gilda* we had Chinese food delivered, but I had already drunk a half-bottle of wine by then, and even though I was sipping, I could feel the effects.

I was pleasantly light-headed when I said goodnight to Michael a little after eleven p.m., leaving him to make his own bed on the living room sofa.

I crashed so hard and slept so soundly that I wasn't at all ready for the ringing phone in the morning.

"So what time are you coming over?" Alicia asked.

Damn.

I struggled to sit up and wished I hadn't.

The hangover wasn't a bad one, as hangovers go. A little nausea and a throbbing pain above my right eye that made me want to leave it shut. As long as I didn't move my head too quickly, the dizziness wasn't bad.

But for the life of me, I couldn't remember telling Alicia that I'd come over.

SIXTEEN

"Why didn't you just say no?" Michael asked, once I was off the phone and we were settled at the kitchen table with lattes in hand. "A lot happened since you apparently told her yesterday that you would come over this morning. Unless you think she made that up."

"I know a lot happened. And I wish I could say I think she made it up, not that I forgot. Anyway, I have to go to the clinic," I argued. "I cancelled my appointments yesterday for good reason, but today I'm functioning again. I can work. And that means I won't be far from where Jimmy and Alicia live, so I might as well stop by on my way in. My visit with them doesn't have anything to do with the murders, just the attack on Alicia and Jimmy's arrest, so whatever we talk about doesn't put me in additional danger. And then when I go to see Natalie, I'll be able to tell her something positive, not just that I'm bailing out on her."

The last point, of course, was the pivotal one. I wasn't looking forward to telling Natalie that I couldn't get her out of jail. Especially since I wasn't convinced that Godines would agree with me that the two murders were connected. Or even if he did, that he could convince a police detective in the proper jurisdiction to reopen Natalie's case.

"I can see that this makes sense to you," Michael said, "but I'm dubious."

"I would be, too, if I were on your side of it. Still, I have to handle it this way."

The look he gave me indicated his disagreement more forcefully than words would have.

"Just do one thing for me," he said. "Keep in mind that this is not a game. You get competitive about games, and you don't want to quit, even when you're losing. Especially when you're losing. But this is life."

"I remember the old joke," I answered. "Games have rules. Life doesn't."

Michael shook his head. "Just remember the fact. What do you want to do about tonight? Since you're going to be on the other side of the hills anyway, do you want to stay with me?" he asked.

I had to ponder that, a task made more difficult by the slight hangover. Was I still frightened? I didn't think so.

"I'll be okay by myself tonight," I told him. "I have to cope with sleeping alone sooner or later, so it might as well be tonight. And I really appreciate everything you did for me yesterday, you know that."

"I know that, but it's nice to hear you say it. Is there anything in your refrigerator that would make a better breakfast than leftover pizza?"

"How about leftover Chinese food?"

"Pizza."

I stuck two slices in the toaster oven to warm up.

We ate the pizza with a second latte, and then I had to rush to get ready to leave.

"You might think of training Amy as a guard cat," Michael said, rinsing out his latte cup. "If she got interested in the idea, Mac would too, and he's big enough to be scary."

"Locking doors, staying out of alleys, and avoiding unfamiliar restrooms is going to have to do it," I told him. "I won't compromise the innocence of my pets, not even for my own safety."

He kissed me on the cheek, and I walked him to the front door, again locking it behind him. As usual. Except that it still felt more important than usual to have locked doors.

I left about fifteen minutes later, having hastily applied makeup and deciding that jeans and sweat shirt would do for the day.

Everybody who lives in L.A. for any length of time learns a little about self-defense. Most of the basic stuff is only useful against strangers, like the admonition to walk as if you know where you're going and what you're doing, and avoid appearing vulnerable. I felt vulnerable, and anyway, if somebody was after me, that somebody wouldn't check the expression behind my dark glasses before attacking.

But the one about keeping your keys in your hand so that you can poke a potential attacker in the eye seemed useful. I walked down to my car prepared to poke. But nobody came near me—almost everyone else in the building had a straight job and had left for it, and there were no strangers lurking.

And the drive to Echo Park was as uneventful as the walk to the car.

Alicia was watching from the front porch as I pulled up and parked. The bruises on her face still looked pretty bad, but the swelling had gone down.

"Hi," I said, hoping for a thanks-for-coming in return.

"Come on in," was all she said.

The living room looked marginally better than it had the last time I was there. Alicia was obviously making an effort here. She had thrown out the dead flowers and tossed a couple of small pillows on the sofa. The heavy drapes were wide open, and enough sunlight made it through the dirty windows that I could see how attractive the furniture would have been in the kind of room it was built for.

"If you need money to pay the rent, sell the furniture," I said.

Alicia looked at me as if I were nuts.

"Jimmy's mom would kill me," she said. "And who would buy it?"

"Advertise it as an estate sale," I told her. "You'll attract dealers. Somebody will buy it. I'll take responsibility with Natalie. Where's Jimmy?"

"Right here." He was standing in the doorway to the hall, half in shadow, and I hadn't noticed him.

Alicia held her hand out, and Jimmy moved close enough to take it. They smiled at each other, for a moment oblivious of my presence. The strength of their connection was so apparent that I could not comprehend how the police had missed it, how officers even as emotionally challenged as Page and Davila

could think for a moment that Jimmy could have
raised his fist against Alicia.

"Have a seat," Alicia said, turning back to me, a
slight glow from within illuminating her bruised face.
"Do you want coffee or anything?"

"No. I don't have a lot of time." I thought about
mentioning the other complications in my life as well,
but there didn't seem to be any point. I sat on the
edge of the sofa and waited.

Jimmy sat in one of the overstuffed chairs. Alicia
draped herself across one arm and the back, almost
like a protective cloak.

"I didn't want to knife the guy," Jimmy said.
When he wasn't looking at Alicia, his face was haggard and pale.

"I believe you. I believed Alicia when she told me
the story," I said. "Is that all you wanted?"

"Oh, wow, lady." He shook his head sadly. "I just
got out of jail, where I sat for two days because nobody would believe I didn't want to knife that dude.
And you're going, is that all I wanted?"

I could give them a few minutes, even if I ran a
little late at the clinic. I leaned back.

"Okay. Tell me the story."

"Alicia said we needed stuff for breakfast, and she
wanted to go to the store before it closed. I told her
to take the car, but she said no, she wanted to walk."
Jimmy clasped his hands on his knees, holding onto
them as if all the joy in his life depended on his grip.

"I did want to walk," Alicia interjected. "It was
a clear night, and the store is only a few blocks. And
the car hasn't been working too good."

I nodded at her, turned back to him. "And what were you doing while she was gone?"

"Watching MTV. Some old dude on *MTV Unplugged.*"

I was afraid to ask who Jimmy thought was an old dude.

"You don't want to hear my side of it again, do you?" Alicia asked.

"That's okay. I remember it," I said. "So what happened next, Jimmy?"

"I heard her screaming, and I went running out into the street, and there she was at the corner, with this guy beating on her. She kept screaming, and he kept slamming her with his fists, and he was, like, a heavyweight dude, and I didn't know what to do." Jimmy had always seemed frail to me. I could understand why he wouldn't want to leap into a fight. "So I pulled my knife, and I shouted at him, 'I've got a knife, dude, let her go. I've got a knife.'"

"But he didn't," I interjected. Jimmy was getting upset, remembering, and I wanted to let him know I was on his side.

"No. He didn't. I kept yelling, 'I've got a knife, dude,' but he didn't stop pounding on her until I stabbed him." Jimmy seemed to shrink in the chair, and Alicia put an arm around his shoulder.

"That stopped him?"

Jimmy nodded. "He was, like, stunned when I pulled the knife out. He dropped Alicia and put his hand on his side and backed away from us, and then he got in his car and left. I helped Alicia back to the house. We were still deciding what we should do, whether we should call the cops, when they showed up here.''

''Where did you get the knife?''

''I gave it to him for his birthday,'' Alicia said. ''Jimmy likes to make things, and I thought he'd like a knife. It's one with lots of tools on it, a corkscrew and stuff.''

''Okay. So you always carry the knife?'' I asked.

''Did,'' Jimmy answered. ''The cops have it now.''

''Did the cops understand that the knife was a gift?''

''No. Those bastard cops, they didn't understand nothing,'' Alicia said.

''I believe you,'' I said. ''Is there anything else I can do for you?''

''Yeah,'' Jimmy sat up straight and looked directly at me. I was struck by how much like Natalie's his sad, dark eyes were. ''You're a psychologist, so I want you to tell me. Why didn't the guy stop beating on Alicia when I told him I had a knife?''

''Oh, God, Jimmy, I don't know,'' I said. ''Maybe he was so caught up in what he was doing that he didn't hear you, or maybe all he could hear was Alicia screaming. Or maybe he just didn't think you'd stab him.''

''Yeah, right.'' Jimmy shrank again. ''He thought I was a wuss, and then the cops think I'm a girlfriend beater. I don't even have to ask you why the cops didn't believe me—I was just another guy with a knife to them. How do I win here?''

''By hanging in,'' I told him. ''You win when you don't give up.''

"Yeah, okay," he said, but he didn't sound convinced, and I wished I had better answers for him, better answers to both of his questions.

Alicia hugged him closer.

"So how are you doing helping my mom?" Jimmy asked.

"Well, I'm kind of at an impasse," I hedged, not wanting to share my problems just then.

"Does that mean you're quitting?" Alicia asked. "You're gonna fuck her over like everybody else?"

"No, no, I'm not fucking her over," I said, feeling my face start to turn red. Alicia's voice reminded me that I had a headache. Or maybe the aspirin was wearing off.

"Then what are you doing?" Alicia asked.

"My best," I snapped at her. "I am doing my best, and a thank you would be in order here, not an attack."

"Okay. Thank you. So what are you doing for Jimmy's mom?" Her lips were set, as if I owed her something for the thank you.

"Going to see her this afternoon," I said. "And I don't have to explain anything to you. Now, if that's all you want, it's time for me to leave."

"You're fucking her over," Alicia said. "Are you going to fuck us over when Jimmy goes to trial?"

"I'm not fucking anybody over. Good-bye."

I picked up my purse and walked out the door.

Jimmy caught up with me on the front porch.

"I'm sorry," he said. "Alicia can be a little rough sometimes. I know you're doing all you can, and my mom knows that, too. You're going to see her this afternoon?''

I wanted to snap at him, but his girlfriend's lousy manners weren't his fault.

"I'll see Natalie sometime today," I said.

"Tell her I'm okay, will you? I just can't face going to see her in jail right now." He made an effort to smile that just made him look sadder.

"I'll tell her you're okay." I held out my hand, and he grasped it in both of his.

"I hope you can get her out of jail soon," he said. "Jail isn't any fun."

"I'm not sure there's anything more I can do," I said, and immediately regretted it. "But I'll try to think of something."

Jimmy nodded and dropped my hand. "Okay."

I got into my car feeling like a lousy human being because I was afraid Alicia was right, that I was fucking Natalie over, despite my protestations to the contrary.

The conversation replayed itself in my head all the way to the clinic. Something was bothering me, and I was going to have to get past the remains of my headache before I could figure out what it was.

In the meantime, I wanted another aspirin.

Mary waved a message slip at me as I walked in the door.

"Call Miriam Stern," she said. "And Nicole is waiting in your office."

"Thank you," I said, dropping the slip in my bag.

I had my priorities straight. First an aspirin, then my appointment with Nicole, then return Miriam

Stern's call. The timing was too suspicious. She must have heard from Godines, and I was in no mood to be chastised again.

The aspirin kicked in halfway through Nicole's hour, so I was feeling alert and painfree when I returned Miriam Stern's call shortly after noon. I was hoping she had already left for lunch, but she hadn't.

And I was right—Godines had called her, and she had her speech for me all set to go.

"What is wrong with you, Faith?" she said, and that was just for starters.

I waited patiently until she had finished telling me—calmly and to great effect—what a total idiot I am.

"I'm sorry," I said, when she finally ended her speech. "I knew I was doing things you didn't want me to do, and I'm afraid you're right. The eavesdropping Debbie Pierce did because I wanted the information got her killed. I can't even begin to tell you how upset I am about that."

"Good. Are you so upset that you're out of this?"

"Sort of," I hedged. "I thought I was out of it until I talked to Jimmy this morning. I have to stay in it enough to get Jimmy through his trial."

"Oh, Faith!"

I cut her off quickly, changing the subject.

"Did Godines tell you how Debbie was murdered?"

"A blow to the base of the skull. Something round and heavy that wasn't left behind. And Godines is a good detective who will do a professional job finding out who did it." Not to be deterred, she added, "Just what do you think you're doing to help Jimmy? And don't play games with me this time.''

"I took pictures of Alicia's battered face, and I said I'd testify that in my expert opinion Jimmy wouldn't hit her. And Jimmy wanted to know why the guy wouldn't stop hitting Alicia when Jimmy threatened him with a knife, something I had no answer for.''

"Some people are a little deaf when it comes to threats," Miriam said.

"Okay. I heard you.'' I also heard my own words.

That was what had been nagging at me, not about me, not about the guy Jimmy knifed, but about Craig Thorson. Craig was a big man, a lot bigger than Natalie. Bigger than Roberta Hill or Jane Browning. Why did he stand there and get knifed? What kind of struggle happened first? Didn't he believe the person with a knife was threatening him?

I wished I could ask Miriam about the crime scene, but I knew she would only blow up at me all over again. The only person who would willingly talk with me about it was Natalie.

And that was one more reason for another trip to Sybil Brand.

"So do you believe the threats now?" Miriam asked, bringing me back to the conversation at hand.

"Yes. I'll go see Natalie this afternoon and tell her what's happened," I said.

"And what else will you tell her?"

"That I've done what I can to help her."

"You're hedging, Faith. Just remember it won't help Natalie if you get yourself killed."

On that note, she said good-bye.

I grabbed a quick lunch from the Cuban bakery and returned for what was a surprisingly encouraging afternoon. Luisa, the client who had been burned out of her apartment, had settled with the insurance company. No lawsuit. She had decided to get on with her life. And Joanna, who was being sued over an auto accident, was ready to admit it was her fault.

Surely that boded well for my trip to Sybil Brand. I left the clinic in relatively good spirits.

By the time I negotiated my way through the interchange to the San Bernardino Freeway, though, I was so tired that I was back to berating myself for Debbie Pierce's death. I steeled myself for a confrontation with Natalie.

The steel turned to slush when Natalie took one look at me and started to sob.

"You have bad news," she said, between deep gasps for breath. "I can tell. Oh, God, Faith, how long do I have to be here?"

"I have some good news first. Jimmy is out of jail, and he said to tell you he's okay." I paused to let that sink in, hoping Natalie would stop crying. When she didn't, I added, "Alicia is looking a little better, and she's doing a good job of taking care of the house."

"Don't tell me about Alicia," Natalie wailed. "It's her fault Jimmy was arrested, and I don't want her living in my house. Get me out of here, please, please, get me out of here."

I sat there and let her cry. I caught the eye of a guard who was looking at Natalie, wondering whether to intervene, and shook my head, letting her know I could handle it. At least I hoped I could handle it. The guard nodded and let her gaze wander on around the room.

When Natalie's sobs subsided to whimpers, I said, "I have to tell you, someone else has been murdered."

"What?" She jerked upright. "Who?"

I told her everything that had been going on, including all the parts I had left out on my earlier visits, which meant the threats. By the time I was done, Natalie had become very small and very quiet.

"You can't help anymore, Faith. I understand," she said. "That poor woman was murdered trying to help, and I won't forgive myself for that. I don't want anything to happen to you."

"But it may be all right," I argued. "Detective Godines seemed to believe me when I told him I thought the murders were related. He called Miriam Stern, so he is following up. This will work out somehow, Natalie."

"Right." Her voice was hollow.

"And even if I can't ask questions of anybody else, I can ask you questions, and there's something you may be able to use to help yourself." I hoped for a reaction, but I didn't get one. "You're a lot smaller than Craig was. Why do the police think he stood still while you knifed him? What do they think happened?"

Natalie's face was blank. "I don't know, what?"

"Think, Natalie. You told me Craig was stabbed in the heart. Was it a single knife thrust? Was there a fight? Were there defensive wounds on his hands and arms?'' The color was beginning to come back into her face, so I kept going. ''Either the murderer surprised him somehow, or he didn't believe the murderer's threats. Or the murderer was bigger than Craig was. And that one, at least, lets you out.''

''How could I have surprised Craig with a knife from his own kitchen?'' Natalie asked.

''I don't know. And you had left threats on his answering machine, so he might have taken it seriously if you grabbed a kitchen knife and came at him.''

''He was a lot stronger than I am,'' Natalie said, beginning to get interested. ''He would have taken the knife away from me. Jimmy, too. Craig was stronger than Jimmy. I'll have to tell Miriam Stern that.''

''Best to leave Jimmy out of it. The guy he knifed was bigger and stronger, but Jimmy managed to do it anyway.''

''Because the guy was too busy beating up Alicia. That's what you said, isn't it?'' Natalie asked.

''Yes.''

''So all you have to do is figure out what Craig was doing when one of those other women knifed him,'' Natalie said. ''And why he didn't really think she'd stab him.''

''All I have to do,'' I repeated.

''Yes. That woman who works out in the gym has to be strong enough, and the prostitute is probably clever enough, and Faith, you haven't even talked to her yet. Don't you think you ought to talk to the prostitute? The one Jimmy saw him with? And then I bet that would do it." Natalie's tears were gone. Hope had returned. "I bet if you just talked to the prostitute, you could figure this whole thing out, without asking any more questions or putting anybody in danger."

"I don't even know how to find the prostitute," I argued. "And Natalie, she may have nothing to do with this, in which case looking for her is a waste of time."

"You could find her. I know you could," Natalie pleaded.

I shut my eyes to think without seeing Natalie's face. If I refused, I'd have to watch her hopes die all over again.

"All right," I said, when I could look at her. "Here's the deal. I'll spend one evening, tonight, looking for the prostitute. And that's the end of my involvement."

"I understand, Faith, I really do, and I appreciate all the help you've given me, and given Jimmy," Natalie said, her face glowing with the hope I couldn't bear to kill. "Come back as soon as you can."

"I'll do my best, Natalie," I said automatically, wondering how many times I had said those words in the last couple of weeks.

I left Natalie in the jail and walked outside into the fading afternoon sun.

All I knew about the hooker was that her name was Tory, she had lots of dark hair, skin the color of a healthy suntan, and Gary Parkman said Craig had brought her to the bar because of some kind of joke. And Debbie said something about Sunset and La

Brea, which was as good a place to start what was sure to be a wasted evening as anywhere else.

Michael had been right when he had said that I don't like to give up, especially when I'm losing, but I was beginning to feel less and less like playing this particular game.

This was life, though, as Michael had reminded me, and I had just promised to play one more round.

SEVENTEEN

"HI, COULD I TALK to you for a second?" I asked for the umpteenth time, approaching two young women with lots of dark hair and some variation of tan or olive or light coffee colored skin who were standing on one of the many corners of Sunset Boulevard that such young women call their own after dark.

After leaving Natalie at Sybil Brand, I had returned to Los Feliz, where I know the restaurants, and stopped for a high carb dinner of eggplant parmesan and bread—great bread—at a little Italian place on Hillhurst. When I had eaten enough to feel fortified for the ordeal, it was only six o'clock, which felt too early to interview hookers. Still, I decided that the sooner I started, the sooner I could call it an evening and go home.

Besides, I had learned in the time I lived near Sunset in Silver Lake that men will stop for a single woman walking along on Sunset any time, day or night, even when her body language makes it clear that she isn't looking for company.

Alicia had learned that lesson, too.

So I started cruising Sunset.

And I found women on the streets, young women, in various modes of dress or undress, some attractive, some not, but many obviously available for a price. When I spotted the first loitering group containing a young woman fitting the description of the one I wanted to talk with, I parked the car and approached on foot.

My pitch was straightforward. I was a therapist from a clinic, and I needed to find a woman named Tory because I had heard she might be in trouble and I wanted to help her. It felt acceptable to me, if a stretch of the truth. I passed out business cards, stayed if somebody had a question, which was always about free therapy, didn't stick around if I was rebuffed.

Nobody knew anybody named Tory, or at least nobody was willing to admit to knowing her.

I had moved the car a couple of times, working my way through Hollywood almost to the edge of the old Sunset Strip, and was feeling saddened by the whole experience when I stopped for what I had decided would be the last two women I would question. Talking with young hookers was so depressing that the only thing that would redeem the evening for me would be the off chance that someone actually would come to the clinic for therapy.

I was also cold. I hadn't left home that morning prepared to work into the evening.

Both of these women had the requisite piles of black curly hair and light brown skin, adorned with multiple silver earrings and bracelets. One was wearing a red velvet dress with spaghetti straps that exposed most of her breasts and some tasteful black floral tattoos on her right shoulder. The other was wearing a T-shirt and jeans with an incongruous pair of black, stiletto-heeled sandals. Neither seemed aware that the evening air was considerably cooler than that of the afternoon.

One more time, I gave them the pitch, working hard to make it sound fresh, and my business card.

"What makes you think Tory is in trouble?" asked the one in jeans.

I was so startled by the response that I said the first thing that came to my mind.

"She might know something about a murder."

The two young women—girls, really—glanced at each other.

"So why would you want to help her if you don't know her?" asked the same one.

"She might be in worse trouble if she talked to you," the other one said.

"Wait—are you telling me that you know her and that she does know something about a murder?" I grabbed the tattooed shoulder as I said it, which was a mistake. Both girls pulled back.

"We didn't say that," the tattooed one said, shrugging me off.

"What is your name?" I asked.

"I'm Jenna Bush, and this is my twin sister, Barbara."

"Okay, Jenna. Listen carefully. One innocent woman is in jail and another innocent woman is dead. If Tory knows something, she isn't safe. If you take me to her, I can see that she gets protection." I would have to think how I could do that, if I did meet Tory, and if she did know something that put her in danger. But one step at a time.

The two girls looked at each other again.

"Tory isn't working the street tonight," the Barbara one said. "But I know her pager number. I could call her."

"Call," I said, pulling out my cell phone and handing it to her.

She took the phone and moved to the side of the nearest building, a high-rise of gray concrete and glass, turning so that I couldn't overhear.

"Are you really a therapist?" the Jenna one asked. "This isn't a scam?"

"I'm really a therapist and this isn't a scam," I said. "I see people at the clinic. You could come by some time and make an appointment, if you wanted to talk."

The Jenna one shrugged. "Maybe."

The Barbara one came back.

"Tory said she'll meet you in an hour, but in a public place, like a coffee shop. Okay?"

"Okay. Does she have one in mind?" I asked.

The Barbara one consulted the phone, clicked it off, and handed it back to me.

"Danny's. On Sunset. It's that way a couple of miles or so." She pointed back the way I had come.

I thanked her, said goodnight, and returned to my car, with mixed feelings.

After all my assurances to Michael and Detective Godines and Miriam Stern that I was through asking questions, I was about to start again. And I couldn't call anyone for help until after I had talked with her, because she might not come into the coffee shop if she saw that I wasn't alone.

On the other hand, there was a chance that Natalie might turn out to be right—that all I had to do was talk to Tory, and Tory would give me the key to the puzzle, the one thing I needed, whatever it was, to figure out what had happened the night Craig Thorson was murdered.

And I couldn't walk away from that possibility.

So I drove back along Sunset to Danny's, which had to be as good a place to wait out the hour as any.

I almost missed it. And when I found it, I almost reconsidered the idea of waiting there. Danny's took up one small space in a row of shops occupying the first floor of a two-story brick building. A locksmith was on one side, a shoe repair place on the other. The second story consisted of some kind of living space— there was a broken security door at the bottom of a stairwell, and a row of mailboxes, which had also been broken into.

The coffee shop itself had room for six tables, five against the wall and one at the front window, and a counter, behind which was a massive grill. Two of the tables were occupied by two teenagers each, all four into heavy grunge. An older African American man sat at one end of the counter, reading a paper as he ate his dinner.

The man behind the counter, a tired, middle-aged Latino wearing a wrap-around apron, looked at me as if I must have stumbled in by mistake.

"I'm meeting someone here," I explained. "Would it be all right if I sat for a while with just a cup of coffee?"

"Sure," he said, sloshing dark coffee into a mug. "Sit anywhere you like."

I took the mug of coffee and poured something from a metal cream pitcher into it. From the sickly gray color the coffee turned, the liquid had to have been milk. I carried the cup to an unoccupied table against the wall and sat down.

Twenty minutes had elapsed since I talked with the girls. I had forty minutes to go before I could expect Tory.

When the older man at the counter finished his dinner about ten minutes later, he left the paper. I got up and retrieved it so that I had something to do other than look at the other people in the coffee shop.

The other half hour elapsed, and I got a refill on my coffee, even though it was burned and bitter and barely drinkable, and the milk didn't help it much. The caffeine so late in the day was starting to make me edgy.

Another ten minutes went by, and I began to think about leaving. But then a young woman came in the door, walked straight to the table, and sat down across from me.

"Who are you and what do you want?" she said.

Tory didn't look like what I had expected, especially after the time I had spent talking to the girls on Sunset. Her thick black hair had been pulled back, twisted into a knot, and caught by a heavy clip under a small blue-and-white scarf. Jimmy had been right about her skin—it was the light brown color that characterizes half of L.A. She hadn't bothered to add makeup or jewelry. In jeans and an LACC T-shirt, she looked like just another community college student, pretty but not exceptional. Except for her eyes.

Her eyes were large and dark and so twitchy that the lids could barely contain them. The rims were red as if she had been crying, and the red had spilled over into the veins of her eyeballs. Her hands twitched, too, and she clasped them firmly together on the table to try to hold them still.

"I'm Faith Cassidy, I want to help you if I can, and if you come to the clinic tomorrow, I could probably get you a prescription for a tranquilizer," I said.

Tory laughed and shook her head.

"You're the third person who's come looking for me in the last two weeks," she said, "and the first one I agreed to meet with. The other two times, the girls didn't even bother to call me. They called this time because you weren't offering money to anybody, only referrals to some clinic."

"Are you freaked out because of something connected with Craig Thorson's murder?" I asked.

"Yes. And I want to know how you're involved."

"I'm involved because his ex-wife was arrested for the murder, and she's my client. I promised her I would try to help." That sounded lame to me as I said it, but I kept my voice and my eyes steady.

Tory closed her eyes, in a vain attempt to control the twitching, then opened them again.

"Tell me what she looks like, the ex-wife."

"Shoulder length dark hair, limp, sad, white face," I said. "Thin frame."

"She didn't do it," Tory said. "I didn't think she was ever his wife, the one who stabbed him."

"Who? Who stabbed him? What happened?" I had to stop myself from reaching across the table to grab her. "Tell me the story."

"If I do, then you aren't safe, either."

"Tory, I'm already not safe. The only way either one of us will be safe again is to get your information to the police so that the people who want to hurt us are in jail," I told her.

"Maybe they'll believe you. I don't think they'd believe me," she said.

"Tell me," I begged. "I'll believe you. And I'll find a way to get the police to believe you."

"Maybe. Anyway, here it is." Tory relaxed, once the decision to talk was made. Her eyes stopped their nervous twitching. "When he picked me up—Craig Thorson—he asked if I was an actress, said he wasn't interested in sex, but he would pay me a lot of money to come with him to a bar, and a lot more money if I would let him fix me up."

"Are you an actress?"

Tory shrugged. "Isn't everybody?"

I didn't bother to answer.

"He didn't give me his real name at the beginning," she continued. "He said I could call him Professor Higgins."

"From *My Fair Lady*," I said. "I had heard from a couple of people at the bar there was some kind of joke involved."

And that reminded me that both Gary Parkman and Debbie Pierce were dead.

"Whatever. So I went with him to the bar, and whatever was going on, the guys were having a good time, all drinking and laughing and everything. Like they thought Craig was really funny.''

"Did they let you in on the joke?" I asked.

"Not then. We had a couple of drinks, and they were all real polite to me, except they were laughing, and then Craig said he'd take me home, but he wanted to pick me up the next day, get my hair done, and a facial and makeup and everything." Tory laughed sharply. "He was going to pay for everything, and pay me for my time. I felt like Julia Roberts or something."

"This was only a few days before he was murdered, right?" I asked.

"Right."

"And then what?"

"Well, I wouldn't let him take me home, because I had a gut feel that I didn't want any of them to know where I lived. I told him where he could drop me off and then pick me up the next day."

"That gut feel is called self-preservation," I said.

"I found that out," she replied. "So anyway, Craig picked me up the next day, and he took me to the Beverly Center and bought me some clothes and then he took me to a place in Hollywood to get my hair and face done. He made sure they taught me to do the makeup, so I could do it for myself."

"A place in Hollywood? It wasn't called Nirvana?"

"No." Tory shook her head. "Nirvana came on Thursday, after he decided he liked the way I handled myself. That was his joke, taking me to Nirvana."

"What happened at Nirvana?"

"Craig told Tamara—if you know Nirvana, I guess you know Tamara—that there was going to be a big ad campaign, and I was going to be the model for it." Her face twisted at the memory. "God, I wanted to believe him."

This time I did reach out. I touched her hand, and she let it curl around mine.

"How did Tamara react?"

"She was cool, as in icy. Showed me around, introduced me to somebody named Jane, and they said whatever I wanted was on the house. But they both stared at me as if something wasn't right. I didn't like either one of them, and I wanted out of there. I went along, playing the part, because Craig was paying me."

"Did you spend much time at Nirvana?"

"Just an hour or so. They left me in the gym and went away somewhere to talk. Then Tamara came to get me, and Craig and I left. He said he needed me again that evening, at his place, and asked if I needed a ride. I told him I could get there on my own." She pulled her hand away and covered her face. Her voice was muffled as she continued. "I had another gut feel, that I shouldn't go."

"But you went," I said.

"Because of the money. I went because of the money."

Her face was still buried.

"Tory, I know this isn't easy for you, but I need to know how Craig was murdered," I said. "We're almost there."

"There," she repeated, raising her head. "There

were three women there, at his apartment, Tamara and Jane and another one, Roberta.''

''I didn't know Roberta was involved with Nirvana,'' I said.

''Tamara and Jane said they wouldn't go along with me as a model for Nirvana unless Roberta agreed,'' Tory said. ''And Roberta started asking me questions, and I got confused. She wanted to know about acting credits, and I didn't know what I was supposed to say.''

''Why hadn't Craig prepared you? Worked out some kind of lie?''

''He had, sort of.'' Her eyes began to fill. ''Craig had said stuff about who I studied with, that kind of thing. But Roberta didn't believe it, and she was asking for details, and I didn't have them.''

''You must have been frightened,'' I said.

''Not then, not yet. I just didn't know what to do,'' Tory answered. ''I knew I was blowing everything, and I didn't know what to do. And then she blew up.''

''Who? Who blew up?''

''Jane. She said she wanted to know what was going on, what kind of game was Craig playing, who was I, and all that. I thought she was going to hit him.''

''What did Craig do?'' I asked.

''Craig laughed. He said I was a hooker, and I was all Nirvana was worth, and that Jane couldn't take a joke.''

''I don't understand the joke.''

Tory shook her head. ''I didn't either. It had something to do with Nirvana not making any money, and Craig not willing to put any more money into it. So he hired a cheap hooker instead of an expensive actress. Nobody thought it was funny except Craig.''

"How did the fight escalate to the point where Jane stabbed him?''

"Oh. No. Jane didn't stab him,'' Tory said, surprised that I had asked that. "Craig said he would get everybody fresh drinks, and he went to the kitchen, and Jane went after him. For a while it was loud, they were arguing about money. Then it got quiet. Tamara got edgy, and then she got up and went into the kitchen, and then there was a scream, and another scream, and Jane said, 'Oh, God, Tamara, what have you done? You've killed him.'''

"Tamara stabbed him?''

Tory nodded. She had looked stressed out when she came into the coffee shop. Now she looked exhausted.

"The other one, Roberta, ran toward the kitchen,'' she said, "and I ran out of the apartment while they weren't paying any attention to me.''

"Then what did you do?''

"I went home. I hid. I've been afraid to work, afraid to do anything, especially after I heard somebody was looking for me.'' Tory looked me straight in the eye. "I'm talking to you because I can't hide forever. What do we do now?''

"Are you sure it was Tamara who stabbed Craig?'' I hedged, because I wasn't sure what we should do now.

"I only know what Jane said. I wasn't in the room,'' Tory answered.

"Do you know who was looking for you?" I asked.

"Tamara or Jane or Roberta was looking for me. A well-dressed blond woman wearing dark glasses. And a guy. Ordinary looking older white guy. That's all I know." Her eyes dropped, as if she had done what she could, and that was it.

Jason Kohl looked pretty ordinary to me. But I had to ask about another white guy.

"Did you ever meet privately with anyone else from the bar? A man named Gary Parkman?" I asked.

Tory shook her head. "I think I remember somebody being called Gary. But I never saw any of the men again."

"Let me see if I can get hold of Detective Godines," I said.

I searched in my bag for my cell phone. When I couldn't find it, I rummaged deeper. Gone.

"Damn. I'm sure I took it back from the woman who called you for me."

"Maybe you did, and maybe you didn't, and maybe somebody lifted it on your way to the car," Tory said.

"Okay." I sighed. "He's probably not available at this time of night anyway, unless I called it an emergency. How about this? Come home with me now, spend the night at my apartment, and in the morning we'll call Detective Godines. We'll go see him together. Maybe we can get you police protection, at least until an arrest is made. Or both of us police protection."

Tory rolled her eyes. "You really want to do that? Take me home with you?"

"You sleep on the couch," I snapped. "I'm tired and I need to get home to feed my cats. Taking you with me means that I don't lose you before I get you to the detective in the morning."

"Okay." She sighed. "Okay. Whatever. I'll sleep on your couch tonight."

I dropped a couple of dollars on the table to make up for having occupied it for so long over a cup of coffee, not that anyone was standing around waiting for it, and slung my bag over my shoulder. Tory followed me out to the car and slid quietly into the passenger seat.

"Why are they after me?" she asked. "I didn't really see the murder. Why don't they let me alone? I wouldn't be talking to you if they had just let me alone."

I concentrated on getting the car away from the curb and into the stream of traffic on Sunset. I was headed east, and a few blocks would take me to the freeway on ramp.

"I don't know," I finally answered. "You are a material witness, and they don't know whether you would have kept quiet or not. Maybe they think you heard more than you remember. Maybe they think you know something about the money Craig and Jane were arguing about."

"But I don't," she said sadly. "I really don't."

We were both too tired to talk much more than that. It was late enough that the freeway moved steadily, and I was off the freeway and onto Moorpark Avenue in record time.

A few minutes later I pulled into my parking spot.

Tory and I trudged wearily up the stairs to my apartment. I had just turned the key in the lock and opened the door when a voice behind me said, "Damn, Faith, I asked you not to make me do this."

I whirled around and found myself facing a man with a gun. But he wasn't Jason Kohl.

The man with a gun was Bill the bartender.

EIGHTEEN

"BILL! WHAT ARE YOU doing with a gun?" I shrieked.

"Get in the apartment and shut up," Bill said, waving his gun at me.

The sound he made came out something short of a snarl, not quite as menacing as he wanted it to be. I thought about arguing with him. But there was that gun waving in his hand. I pushed Tory inside the apartment and stepped in after her.

Bill followed, shutting the door without taking his eyes, or his gun, off me.

Amy took one look at him and headed for the bedroom, dinner forgotten. Mac was right behind her.

The cats having sense enough to hide was the best thing that had happened to me all day.

"Shit, lady," Tory said. "I guess you aren't going to protect me after all."

First I had to protect me. Looking at the gun was slightly disorienting, as if it were a scene out of a movie. And if this were a movie, then I would have to survive. I couldn't be killed.

In the movie, Catherine Zeta-Jones would play me, and Julia Roberts would play Tory. Tory would like that. I imagined Catherine Zeta-Jones with a sword in her hand, from *The Mask of Zorro,* flicking the gun away from Bill.

I held on to the image of Catherine Zeta-Jones and summoned whatever little bits of star power were hiding in my psyche to deal with the situation.

"I don't understand," I said to Bill, ignoring Tory. My voice didn't waver. I began to feel better, hearing it. "You didn't kill Craig Thorson. You didn't kill Debbie Pierce. Or at least I don't think you did. So what are you doing threatening us with a gun?"

"Helping them is the only chance I got to keep the bar," he said, sighing. "The financial thing got really complicated. With Thorson dead, and his ex-wife in jail, nobody's going to look too closely at Thorson's dealings. And that way the bar is mine. But Jane says that if Tamara goes down for murder, and they lose Nirvana, she'll see that I lose the bar."

"The bar. Halloran's. You own Halloran's?" I asked.

"Officially. Unofficially, Craig Thorson—and maybe some other people—had a half interest," he answered. "But Jane said she'd make sure the bar was mine if I made the questions about Thorson go away. It's a plus for me that you found the hooker."

Suddenly the phone rang, startling all of us.

"Let the machine get it," Bill said.

We stood there, staring at the machine on my desk, until it answered the call and cycled through the outgoing message.

"Hi, Faith," Michael's voice said, with a touch of annoyance. "Give me a call when you get home."

"Who was that?" Bill asked when the machine clicked off.

"A friend. Nothing important." I wondered whether, if I had dashed for the phone and screamed into the receiver, Bill would really have shot me. Catherine Zeta-Jones would have acted. I had just blown my chance.

"We might as well sit down," Bill said, gesturing toward the sofa.

"Why?" I asked. "What happens next?"

"We're waiting for Jane. I called her on my cell phone when I saw you coming up the stairs with the hooker."

"Okay," I said, pulling my desk chair around and sitting there. I was still thinking about a grab for the phone, rehearsing it in my head. "Then while we're waiting, you can tell us the whole story. Start with how Thorson came to unofficially own half your bar. Halloran's obviously makes money. Why did you need an investor?"

"I don't believe you!" Tory's eyes had started twitching again, and the rest of her body wasn't far behind. "This guy's threatening to shoot us, and you want his life story?"

"Sit down, Tory," I said, as calmly and professionally as I could manage. "Yes. I do want to hear his life story."

I also wanted to point out to her that he wasn't going to shoot as long as he was talking. I could do that later.

Tory dropped onto the sofa, hugging herself, and Bill sat in the overstuffed chair next to it, the one I usually reserved for myself when clients were here. He was still holding the gun on me, but not with any sense of urgency in the grip.

"Halloran's does make money," he said. "But I went through a divorce, and I needed cash. Thorson offered it, with enough to pay for some improvements as well. I liked the idea, and then I found myself signing some papers, without an attorney, because Thorson didn't want anybody to know. He put cash in a corporate account that I could draw on, in a bank where Gary Parkman was some sort of officer. This was about two years ago, and everything was fine for the first year, but then he had his own divorce to go through, and he wanted money back, more than I had available. I skimmed off some cash from receipts, but he wanted more. We had a big fight about it. I told him to back off or I'd tell about the cash bank deposits."

"Bill, you don't happen to own a Porsche, do you?" I asked.

"Yeah, why?"

"Never mind." One question answered. Bill was the man in the Porsche Jimmy had seen arguing with Craig. In fact, a second question was answered. If Gary Parkman was helping Thorson hide assets, of course he wouldn't want questions about it.

"I think maybe it was then he brought Jane in, sold her a piece of his investment in the bar. Anyway, when you started asking questions, I mentioned it to Jane. I told her you were talking to Parkman, and God help me, I told her maybe Debbie was eavesdropping to help you." His eyes filled with tears as he thought about Debbie, but he quickly blinked them away. "Jane had already asked me to find the hooker. Now she wanted me to get you off her back. She said I'd lose the bar if I didn't help her."

"Tory said it was Tamara who knifed Craig Thorson, not Jane. Why is Jane doing all this for Tamara?" I asked.

"You'll have to ask her," Bill said.

I hoped I wouldn't have to do that. I had my fingers crossed that the police could do it for me.

"How could Jane cause you to lose the bar?" I asked.

"She said if she made the whole thing public, I'd get in trouble for skimming money, trouble for accepting the cash in the first place, and that Thorson had so many creditors the bar might be seized to pay them." Bill shook his head sadly. "I wish I hadn't gotten into any of this. She also said she could borrow money against her share of the bar and then turn it over to creditors, if she really wanted to make trouble for me. She talked about lawyers, too, and I knew it would be too much for me to handle, that I would lose the bar one way or another."

"So what have you done to help Jane besides make threatening phone calls to Debbie and to me and look for Tory on Sunset?" I asked, adding quickly, "Until tonight, I mean."

"Until tonight, nothing else." His jowls sagged as he said it.

"And I know you didn't want Debbie murdered. Was that Tamara too?" I asked.

"Yeah. Debbie walked into the ladies room just in

time to catch something Jane said, enough for her to put some of the pieces together. Tamara realized it, and she blew. She pulled a hand weight out of her bag, and hit Debbie so hard she killed her. Jane kept other women away somehow—Jane could do it—while Tamara hid the body in the stall." He looked up at me, pleading. "I didn't know. When I asked you to look for her, I really thought maybe she just got sick."

"I believe you." I leaned forward and lowered my voice. "Let's call the police."

My heart lurched. I thought of Catherine Zeta-Jones and kept my voice steady.

"Sooner or later this will unravel," I continued. "Jane and Tamara will get caught, and you with them. Better to blow the whistle now."

"I'll lose the bar," Bill said in barely more than a whisper. "And the bar is my life."

"Maybe you don't have to lose it," I argued, knowing he surely would. "If you tell the police everything you know, maybe you can work something out. You got caught up in this, and it started innocently. I can help you explain that."

"Oh, lady," Tory said, shaking her head.

I glared at her, willing her to keep out of it.

"What do you say, Bill? If you put the gun away now, I won't even mention it to the police. And neither will Tory," I added desperately.

Tory had the grace to keep her mouth shut.

"I don't know," Bill said, looking at the gun in his hand.

He was wavering, and I think I could have convinced him to drop the gun and let me call the police if I'd only had another minute to talk.

But just then there was a knock at the door, and the gun was once again pointing at me.

"See who it is," he said.

I got up and checked the peephole.

Jane and Tamara were standing there.

"I don't have to let them in," I said quietly, turning so that my back was against the door. "You're not a killer, Bill, and I don't think you'd shoot me."

"Maybe not," he said. His whole face was sagging now, like a hound who had lost the scent. "But I'd hit you if I had to, Faith. So let them in."

That wasn't a bluff. I opened the door.

"Good evening, Faith," Jane said. "I know you won't mind if we come in. We won't stay long. Although we may ask you to come with us when we leave."

"Why are you so intent on protecting Tamara?" I asked, blocking the entrance.

"Let us in now," Jane said calmly. "I won't discuss this on the doorstep."

I backed down and let them in.

"Why are you protecting Tamara?" I asked again, after shutting the door behind them.

"The simple answer is that Tamara is my cousin," Jane said. "Beyond that, there is the financial loss I would incur if all of Craig Thorson's dealings, and my involvement in them, came to light. My attorney gets enough money now. I have no desire to personally fund her retirement account."

Seeing the two of them standing side by side, I

could see the family resemblance. I hadn't noticed it before because so many L.A. women of a certain age and social class affect such a similar style. The wealthy crones as clones. If Jane said Roberta Hill was her cousin, I would have to believe that, too.

"You were involved with all of Thorson's complicated finances," I said. "So you must have been connected with Gary Parkman, too. Is that why you killed him? To keep your financial dealings quiet?"

Jane's carefully plucked eyebrows lifted in surprise. The question surprised me, too. I didn't know I was going to ask it until it came out.

"Gary had a heart attack," Jane said, eyebrows back in place, voice calm. "I had only planned to engage his support. I didn't expect him to die. It seems, though, that I inadvertently helped the heart attack along with a little too much Viagra."

"Stop this," Tamara said, drawing the final sound into a hiss. "We don't need to talk about what's happened. Whatever we're going to do now, let's get on with it."

"What *are* you going to do?" I asked. "Kill me too? And Tory? How many bodies are you going to pile up? What about Bill? At what point do you turn on him?"

I didn't bother to look at Bill, but I heard the sharp intake of breath.

"I won't talk," Tory moaned softly from the sofa. "Just let me go, and I promise I won't talk."

"That's probably true," Jane responded. "But if Faith could find you, so could someone else, especially if that someone knew Faith was looking for you when she disappeared. And I'm sorry, Faith, but you do need to disappear.''

"And Bill?" I asked.

"I won't turn on Bill because Bill won't turn on me," Jane said. "I've promised to make certain that he regains full title to Halloran's, free and clear, and I can only do that if I'm free and clear."

"Let's go," Tamara said. "I don't like this."

"You wouldn't," I said. "You started it. One last question. What happened in the kitchen? Why did you stab Craig Thorson?"

Jane and Tamara exchanged swift glances.

"It seems we were sharing more than we knew," Jane said.

"Craig was screwing both of you," I said. "But only his buddies at the bar knew, and they thought the other woman was Roberta, not Tamara. Their mistake. Craig made several, the last of which was that he was starting to get it on with you in the kitchen when Tamara was in the living room. Tamara came in and realized what was going on. Craig didn't know she had picked up a knife until it was too late. That's why he didn't struggle.''

"Let's go," Tamara said again.

I was out of delaying actions, and I didn't know what good they would do anyway. Whatever resourceful move Catherine Zeta-Jones could come up with was beyond me.

Jane's reassurance that Bill would get his bar seemed to have strengthened his tie to her. He was standing now, gun pointed at me still, even though he didn't seem very happy about it.

"How do we do this?" he asked.

"We'll take my car," Jane said. "The three of them in the back seat, Tamara in the middle. I'll drive, and you keep the gun ready in case Faith tries something stupid."

"Where are we going?" I asked. If I knew where we were going, there was still a slim chance I could figure out something not stupid that would get us out of the car before we got there.

"To the Marina," Jane said. "I have a boat there. A little night cruise. You'll fall overboard, and unfortunately we won't be able to save you. And since hookers disappear all the time, we won't bother to come up with a story about Tory."

Tory didn't respond. She had subsided into a kind of glazed stupor.

Tamara grabbed her and pulled her to her feet.

"Come on," she said.

Jane opened the door and indicated with a sweep of her arm that we were to leave. First Tamara with Tory, then Bill with the gun in one hand and my elbow in the other, then Jane.

Jane's white Mercedes was parked just down the street. I looked around, hoping to see somebody I could alert to what was happening, but nobody was taking a late evening stroll.

We got into the car, exactly as Jane planned.

I began to think that not even Catherine Zeta-Jones could get out of this one.

I shut my eyes, wondering how I could prepare for death.

Jane started the engine, and I opened my eyes

again, just in time to see what happened next. She had begun to pull out of the parking space when a dark car came hurtling down the street and crashed into the driver's side of the front end, pinning the Mercedes against the rear fender of the car that had been parked in front of it.

My head hit the window, and I blanked out for a minute. When sight and sound registered again, I could hear sirens.

I could also see Michael's face against the glass, and hear his voice screaming, "Are you all right? Are you all right?"

NINETEEN

"CATHERINE ZETA-JONES?" Michael asked. "You imagined you would be played by Catherine Zeta-Jones?"

"Well, she would need to agree to blond highlights," I said.

"Why not Lucy Lawless? Go all the way with Xena?"

"Because she would have let out a warrior yell and kicked the gun out of his hand," I explained. "Not in my wildest fantasies could I kick a gun out of someone's hand."

It was Saturday, and we were sipping iced tea at a small restaurant on Ventura Boulevard in Encino, sitting outside at a table under a tree, on a slate covered patio dotted with lush, blooming geraniums and tall space heaters. Talking to the police had taken up much of Friday, and I was still so stressed out by the events on Thursday night leading up to the car accident that I cancelled my Saturday appointments as well. So in one more gesture of unconditional love, Michael had driven over to the Valley to comfort me. Comfort, to both of us, included food.

In truth, the love wasn't totally unconditional. He needed to talk.

"Well, your Catherine Zeta-Jones fantasy at least kept you in the apartment making them talk until I got there," Michael said. "I had left three or four messages for you, and I began to get nervous when you didn't call me back, even having visions of your battered body on the floor, so I finally decided I had to drive over to make certain you really weren't home. I was looking for a parking place when I saw the five of you walking along the sidewalk. I didn't see the gun, but I knew something was wrong from the way you were being herded. I called 911 on my cell phone, and thank God they answered right away. All I could do was scream out the address and hit the gas pedal. I am so thankful you weren't hurt."

That was the fourth or fifth time he had told me the same story. And it was the first time in the years I had known him that I could remember Michael being more frazzled than I over something. If it weren't for that, and if he hadn't rescued me, I would have been annoyed at having to listen, at our roles in the friendship being reversed, especially since I was the one who could have been killed. As it was, I listened patiently.

"I know you were terrified," I told him. "But it worked out perfectly. You saved me from being tossed into the Pacific Ocean, and Jane was the only one hurt. I had mixed feelings when I heard it wasn't serious, that she'll recover in time to stand trial."

"What did the police tell you?"

"Not much. Police officers are always better at getting information than giving it. Insisting on talking to

Detective Godines helped a little. I didn't have to work to establish my credibility,'' I answered.

"Tell me what they said," Michael pleaded. "I'm going to be sued for causing that accident, you know that, and my best defense goes down the tubes if they can't hold on to your abductors."

A young waiter in white shirt and slacks appeared beside the table, pad and pencil poised.

"Are you ready to order?" he asked.

"Food first," I said, unable to resist, after all the times Michael had made me wait.

"I'll have whatever she's having." Michael sighed.

"The grilled ahi burger." I smiled at the waiter, who smiled back and left.

"What did Godines tell you?" Michael asked.

"The police can hold all three of them, Jane, Tamara, and Bill, on kidnapping charges while they continue to investigate the murders. Fortunately, Tamara had a hand weight in her bag that was the right size and shape to be the weapon used to kill Debbie."

"Wasn't she smart enough to get rid of it?"

"It's one of a pair, the kind you carry when you walk. You swing your arms with the weights in your hands." I said. "I guess she got rid of one but not the other."

"There's still a lot for the police to put together," Michael replied.

"I know. But they have all the pieces. Craig Thorson was siphoning funds into a phony business account at the bank where Gary Parkman was a vice president, helping him cover the trail. From there, he was making investments that didn't have his name on any official papers. The bank records will give the attorneys a lead on Thorson's hidden assets, which included interests in Nirvana and Halloran's.'' I paused for a sip of iced tea. ''The two big mistakes Thorson made came from overweening arrogance. He was screwing both Jane and Tamara, a bad move to start with, and then he couldn't resist parading a hooker in front of them, making fun of them and their beloved spa, Nirvana, as well.''

''Do you think your friends Bill and Tory will tell what they know? And then actually testify?''

I made the appropriate face at the thought that either Bill or Tory was a friend.

''I suspect Bill will cut a deal for his testimony,'' I said. ''He really didn't do much except help with the cover up. And Tory made an appointment to see me at the clinic on Tuesday. I'll know more after I've talked with her then—although I won't be able to tell you, of course.''

''You won't be able to tell me?'' Michael was genuinely surprised. ''When did I stop being your consulting therapist?''

''When you got involved in this too. You have a stake—Tory could sue you for the accident, you know—so you can't be a consultant. Sorry,'' I told him.

''I was saving her life,'' he argued.

''I know. And she may be grateful, especially after a little therapy to help her see she has a life worth saving. And besides, you don't have much in the way of assets. Except, of course, for Elizabeth.'' I smiled.

"You can smile," Michael responded. "You're off the lawsuit hook."

"At least that much of it worked the way I hoped," I said, letting a fleeting thought of Debbie Pierce's dead body pass through my mind. "Miriam Stern called me last night. She had talked to Godines, and she said he'll work with her to get the charges against Natalie dropped. She also said that the ADA who is prosecuting Jimmy has had second thoughts after seeing Jimmy and Alicia together and interviewing Alicia alone. So Natalie will have a happy homecoming. Jimmy out of jail and the possibility of some of Craig's money, if there is any left after the attorneys and the creditors get through with the assets."

"It doesn't sound as if she was mad at you, anyway," Michael said.

"Well, she wasn't happy. I had to admit that I hadn't been prudent, but she had to admit that I helped her client."

"Was the outcome worth the cost?" Michael asked, picking up on the lack of good cheer under the words.

"If not for Debbie's death, I'd say definitely. Now, I'll have to think about it."

The waiter placed our sandwiches in front of us with a flourish.

"Enjoy your lunch," he said.

"I think I will," I told him.

"Because both of us need a change of subject," Michael said as he added some Dijon mustard to the bun, "do you think this is really the end of your relationship with Richard?"

"I don't know. If he invites me to the gallery opening, I might go. I really do respect his talent, and I want to see how that painting turned out." I sliced the burger in half and prepared to eat.

"And then what?" Michael asked.

"I don't know. I really don't know," I put the burger half down again. "Richard doesn't seem to have much to do with my life anymore. I became a therapist to help people, and then I got hooked on the adrenaline rush of really helping them, getting them out of trouble. I got into this whole mess to help Natalie, and to help myself, too, of course. I did that, but it cost Debbie's life. I think I may just need to be quiet for a while, see what my life feels like when it's quiet."

"I'll believe that when I see it," Michael said. "But in the meantime, I'll drink to it."

He lifted his glass of iced tea, and I clinked mine against it.

I took a sip, and I shivered.

The weather had shifted. The first storm of the winter was about to break over our heads.

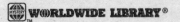

DESERT

BETTY WEBB

NOIR

A LENA JONES MYSTERY

Clarice Kobe is found beaten to death and her ex-husband is the prime suspect. Lena Jones thinks there's more to the murder of her neighbor. Knowing Clarice had a darker side, Lena follows her suspicions to a deadly showdown.

Lena's search for Clarice's killer leads her into a depraved world where love and hate are interchangeable. As she closes in on a killer, she will be forced to make a final choice between acceptance and fear, between life and death, between leaving this world...or embracing it.

"A must read for any fan of the modern female PI novel."
—*Publishers Weekly*

Available October 2003 at your favorite retail outlet.

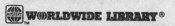

WORLDWIDE LIBRARY®

WBW470

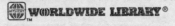